EGYPTUS

And Ham, Son of Noah

THE SONS OF NOAH Vol 1

Young Adult Version

(Children's Version also available)

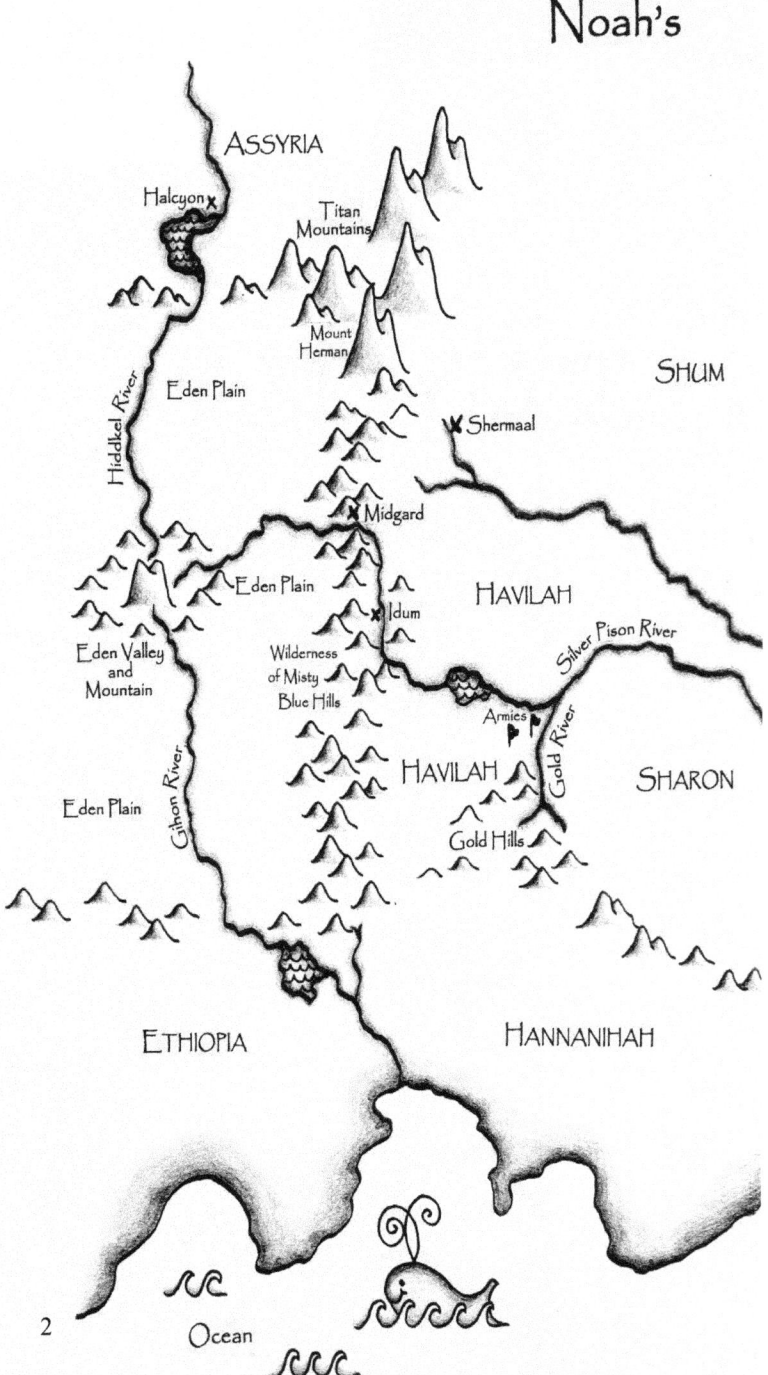

Noah's

ASSYRIA

Halcyon

Titan Mountains

Mount Herman

SHUM

Eden Plain

Hiddkel River

Shermaal

Midgard

Eden Plain

HAVILAH

Idum

Eden Valley and Mountain

Wilderness of Misty Blue Hills

Silver Pison River

Armies

Gold River

Eden Plain

Gihon River

HAVILAH

SHARON

Gold Hills

ETHIOPIA

HANNANIHAH

2

Ocean

Map

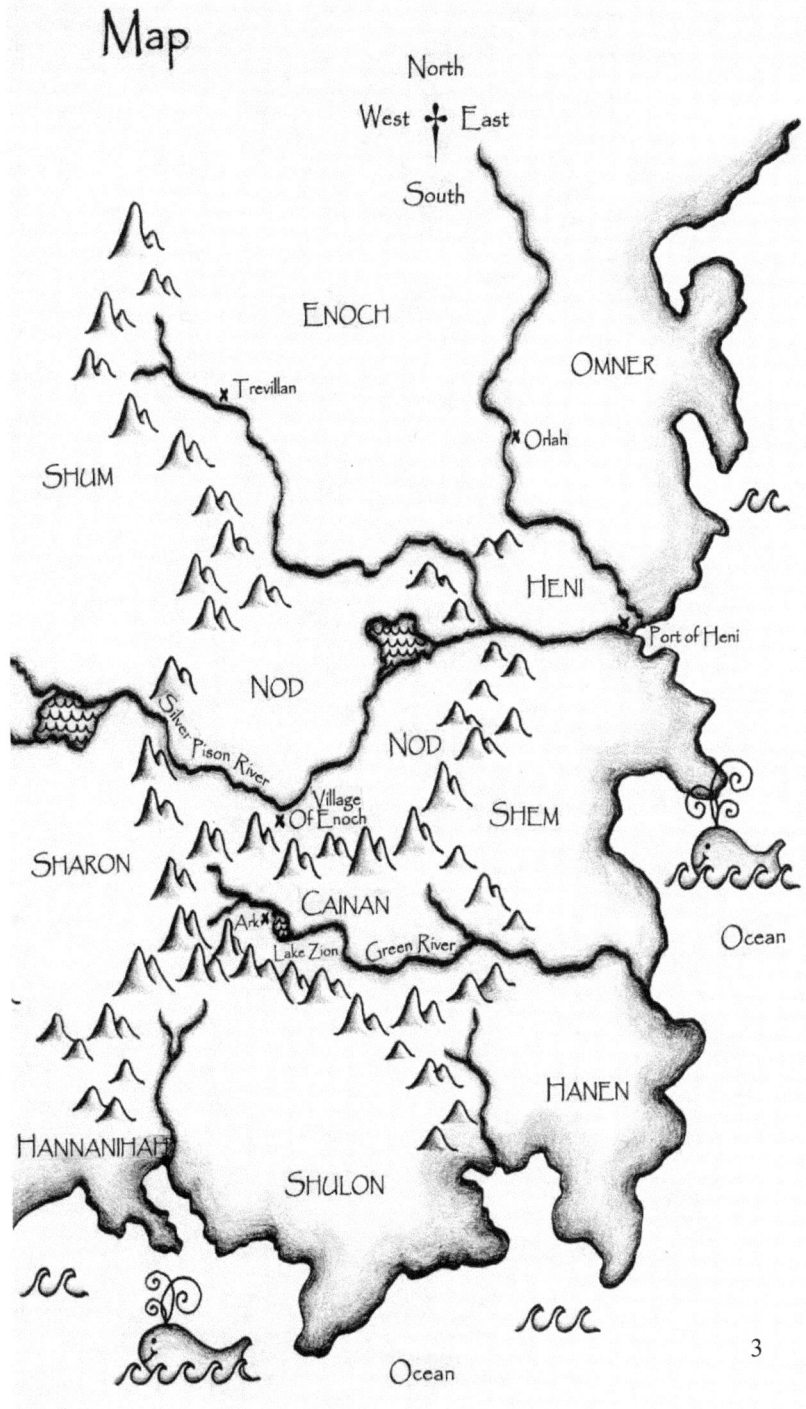

North
West · East
South

ENOCH

OMNER

x Trevillan

SHUM

x Orlah

HENI

Port of Heni

NOD

Silver Pison River

NOD

Village
Of Enoch

SHEM

SHARON

CAINAN

Ark x
Lake Zion

Green River

Ocean

HANNANIHAH

HANEN

SHULON

Ocean

EGYPTUS

And Ham, Son of Noah

M.M. Robison

Illustrated by Melanie A. Murphy

Illiterate Giraffe Publishing LLC
Salt Lake City, U.S.A.

© 2014 Melanie A. Murphy

First printing 2014

Visit us at MMRobison.com

While a number of the characters who appear in this book are based on historical figures and events that happened, it is important to stress that this story is a work of fiction for your enjoyment, that the portraits of the characters who appear in it are fictional, and the tenets are to support the story, not represent any singular Faith.

Library of Congress Cataloging-in-Publication Data

ISBN 10: 0991384008
ISBN 13: 978-0991384006

Robison, M.M.
      Egyptus, and Ham, Son of Noah / M.M. Robison
      (The Sons of Noah; v. 1)
      Includes bibliographical references
1. Fiction/Romance/Fantasy. 2. Fiction/Action & Adventure.
3. Fiction/African American/Historical.

Printed in the United States of America

This Story is for all of the actors, artists, authors, and musicians (living and dead) who have entertained and inspired me.

Thank you for laboring to create what only you can.

The world is richer because of you.

Chapter One

HAM: "You need a wife. Soon," Father says, staring intently at me.

"I know." My shoulders sag. We're almost done loading the horses and mules, then we're off on what might be our last trading trip before the flood comes. I look at Father. "I want to marry Egypt."

"I know you do," he sighs, sharing my frustration. "You'll figure something out. God will provide." Noticing Jarom needs help, he hurries over to help secure a heavy bundle onto a mule.

I finish loading my pack onto Thor, brooding over the barriers between Egypt and me. If I'd had my way, we'd have been married years ago. Finally I pat Thor's neck.

"God will have to provide." Thor nuzzles my head, then nickers reassuringly.

EGYPTUS: It's a very good dream, the kind I'd like to have every night: I'm walking to market with mother, my little warm hand in hers. A few palace servants follow behind us, ready to pay for and carry our purchases. The servants could have gone to market for her, but mama insisted on going herself. She said it kept her in touch with the people, and as their queen, she needed to know what was going on. But I watched her stroking the smooth silks, smelling the fresh fruit, trying on the pretty jewelry and hats. She couldn't fool me. The queen just loved to shop.

Now I lie awake in my warm bed gazing into the dark. I've probably had that dream because today is market day and I love to shop too, especially in the spring when *he* comes -- my tall, lean, talented Ham.

I roll over and consider the possibility that he'll come today. The deer herds have gone back up the slopes, after wintering down here below. The pass between our valley of Nod and his Cainan valley *might* be melted enough for him to get through.

I'll get ready just in case. I've got plenty of time to bathe in scented water, and put on my new yellow gown and mama's dangling earrings, the ones with the green stones. This could be the week he'll come.

If only papa weren't so possessive, and if only our tribes could intermarry. Maybe in the next few centuries things will change and the barriers between us will fall.

HAM: The sky is just beginning to lighten as we crest the mountain pass. Then there it is spread out before me: the most beautiful place on mortal earth, at least to my love laden eyes -- Egyptus' home -- the broad valley of Nod. The horses and I pause for a minute to look out over the valley from our lofty perch on top of the mountain. Our frosty breath creates tiny versions of the puffy clouds hanging at our level across the sky.

Snow-capped mountains ring the valley. Cities and fields are sleeping quietly as morning alights. There are dozens of emerging greens, interrupted by drifts of pink and white where the fruit trees are bursting in bloom.

I look for the palace where my tall, dark, beautiful princess probably still lies asleep. There it is below me and to my left. Egyptus' home is broad and low, with pillared porches surrounding its four sides. Outbuildings and a massive stone wall enclose it. From this height it looks tiny, nestled in surrounding orchards and fields.

The sight of it makes me even more eager to be there with her. I want to carry Egyptus away with me and spend the next few centuries loving her.

Father and the rest of the trading party are slower than my horses and me. They will follow soon, their horses and mules laden with fine cloth and other quality goods that the residents here eagerly await. I hope Egyptus is eagerly awaiting me, and not just for the strong horses I have to sell.

As we descend toward the palace, my heart seems to thud as loudly as the horses' hooves. Maybe this will be the year that her father Nehor will say "yes."

NEHOR: Light spills into the room as my daughter Egyptus joins me in the royal dining hall.

"Good morning papa," she says, sliding onto the bench across from me at the long table, while looking out the window. The light falls on her high cheekbones and full lips. Her thick, black hair has been twisted up and is secured by a yellow band wrapped around her head. She looks regal. And beautiful.

I follow her gaze out the window. This room is pleasant in the morning, with its view of the eastern mountains and sunshine.

Adah, the palace chef, enters the room and lays out cheese and bread. In a couple months it will be summer and we'll have fresh fruit and vegetables again. At least we already have mint leaves, steeped into tea. Adah pours me a steaming cup, then she adds a spoonful of honey. It smells delicious.

Being the king has its privileges. I love good food, good wine, and the best of everything; including Egyptus, who is the best daughter ever. She's so much like her mother, who was also named Egyptus. She runs the palace, charms visiting dignitaries and peasants alike, and keeps me company. I'm not about to part with her. She looks especially nice today, dressed in a yellow gown decorated with green embroidered flowers over matching green leggings. She looks like spring. And like she's lost in her thoughts.

"It's market day, isn't it?" I ask.

"Yes," she says, spreading soft goat cheese on her bread roll. She's smiling absently and begins stirring her tea.

I try for her attention again. "Looks like a pretty day today."

"Yes." She takes a bite of her bread and begins to chew slowly, looking out the window toward the mountain pass.

Hmmm. Spring. Ham comes this time of year. "I need a new horse this year, maybe two."

She finally looks at me and grins. "Ham sells the best horses."

"Yes," I agree.

Adah looks up. "Ham is in the courtyard waiting to see you. He has some mighty fine stallions this year."

Egyptus and I look at each other. "Send him in," we say together, and Adah goes to fetch him. Egyptus stops eating. I start.

Soon Adah returns followed by Ham -- tall, fair, and windblown. He greets me and bows, then looks at Egyptus and bows to her. They look into each others' eyes. What they see pleases them. Obviously.

Silence. Awkward. I clear my throat for attention. "So, Ham. I hear you bring superior horses this year."

Ham looks at me. Finally. "Yes, sir. I believe they are my best yet: big, strong, very well trained."

"They always are."

"I do my best." His eyes stray back to Egyptus, who is motionless now, blushing and looking down at her half-eaten bun and cheese.

I look at the two unsuited suitors and sigh. We go through this every spring and sometimes in the fall, when Ham and his family come through the valley to trade. They are a likable bunch, and honest for traders. After market his father Noah will preach before packing up and moving on. Sometimes he'll stay and preach for two or more evenings before they leave. Occasionally the father's sermons will anger the crowd, but his crew knows how to pack and get out of town quickly.

They travel to all the valleys and kingdoms. Probably everyone in the world has heard his pontificating. Crazy old man. Like anyone is going to listen. We all like our wine, women, and song too much to change. 'Follow the One God' indeed. Nope.

I motion to Ham to sit with us. He does, folding his long body onto the bench beside my daughter. I try to refocus his attention. "I was just telling Egyptus that I could use one or two more good horses this year." She looks up at Ham and nods.

He grins down at her. "You know you can have them all in exchange for Egyptus' hand." He winks at her. "She's at least an eight horse wife." She blushes again and looks back at her plate.

So much for refocusing. I sigh again. Like I said, we go through this every year. "Well, I can't part with Egyptus this year, but I will look at your stallions. I'd like to buy Thor too, of course."

He smiles at me and shakes his head. "Well, I can't part with Thor this year, but I'll let you have one or two of his offspring. Shall we go take a look at them?"

Egyptus tries to hide her smile and follows us out to the courtyard. Ham's not getting *my* offspring. Our tribes don't intermarry. Even if they did, a king's daughter doesn't belong with a preacher's son. Or a trader's.

EGYPTUS: Papa and Ham chat as we head to the courtyard. The two men are the same height, but otherwise opposites. Papa is dark, massive, and muscular. Ham is light, strong, and fast. Papa would probably win in a fistfight, but Ham could outrun or outride him, and is rumored to be an excellent swordsman, so he'd be in no danger.

They are both very intelligent, with papa being more cunning, but Ham is quicker to assess others and solve problems. He's also exceedingly reliable and very persistent. Papa generally enjoys Ham's company, as Ham is not only a good listener, but is well-traveled and always has news of other kingdoms.

I overhear Ham say that his mother is well. She's not with the trading party this year. Papa says Nod is thriving this spring. The mild winter helped.

We step into the courtyard and papa's eyes brighten. These are indeed fine horses. As fine as any ever seen.

Thor stands a head taller than his sons. His grey coat is almost too shiny to be real, his eyes too bright, his rump too round and muscular: an animal not to be forgotten. Ham keeps his breeding mares and foals in Cainan, his home valley. But Thor goes everywhere with him, like a very large, devoted dog.

The two men are circulating among the stallions. Papa bends to pat a flank. Ham shows him a noble set of teeth on a large black stallion. Papa nods. Ham smiles, flashing his own set of fine teeth. Everything about Ham is fine -- his straight nose, strong jawline. His blue eyes have a hard time remaining solemn when there's humor to be found in any situation. He looks so young. Maybe it's his hair: thick, blond, longish. I like how it curls on the back of his neck. Maybe it's his lack of beard, just stubble today. Must have been in a hurry this morning.

While I'm musing over Ham and his many virtues, Papa has chosen the black stallion and they've negotiated a price. It's a very expensive horse, the finest of the lot.

Papa turns to me. "I can't ride right now, I have to stay here, of course." He's referring to the fact that it's Judgement Day, which is always on the first market day of the month for everyone's convenience. Anyone who needs the king's advice or judgement in a dispute can show up. Papa must stay to arbitrate.

He continues, "Would you like to try out this horse for me and make sure he's worth the price? If he is, Ham can return this afternoon for payment."

I nod. Of course I will. I'm already in love with the stallion. Anything Ham breeds and trains, I love. "I'll ride him to market, papa, then over the fields on my way home."

"Okay. Remember your uncles are coming tonight."

"Yes, papa. I'll make sure your dinner is ready early this evening, then leave for town. I want to hear the preaching tonight." Or rather, I want to sit with Ham and hear the preaching tonight.

Papa seems to read my thoughts and gives me a look that says I'd better behave myself. I nod in acknowledgement and he nods back then leaves us, going up the steps and through the front doors. He knows that I am perfectly safe with Ham. Even animals trust him.

I look at Ham and our eyes meet again. A shiver of warmth goes through me.

Ham finally steps forward with the black stallion.

"He's beautiful," I say. "What's his name?"

"Midnight. Night for short. Not a very original name for a black horse, I know."

"It suits him though."

"He's very fast. And very smart, aren't you boy?" Ham reaches up and pats Night on the cheek. Night nuzzles him back.

I observe, "He likes you. He'll miss you."

Ham nods. "I'll miss him too, but one can only feed so many horses. He needs to move on, make his own life, breed with his own mares."

17

Night's large black eye is examining me. I reach out and touch his neck. "Hey boy, shall we go for a ride?" Midnight nuzzles Ham's head again as if to show his preference of riders.

Ham laughs and shrugs. "Maybe we should ride him together this first time."

Being that close to Ham sounds heavenly. I grin and look at Night's broad back. "Well... if you're sure there's enough room for both of us."

"I believe there is."

"Let me get my boots on and I'll be ready."

Ham grins as I run up the steps and through the front door. Kicking my slippers off, I grab my tall brown boots from my room, hopping into them as I hurry back out, while wrapping my green coat around me for warmth. In the half-minute I've been gone, Ham has led the horses out of the courtyard onto the path leading to town.

HAM: As Egyptus hurries toward me my heart melts. Everything about her appeals to me. On the outside she's heartbreakingly beautiful and alluringly tall, coming up to my nose. Inside, her nature is gentle and good. She always seems so graceful to me, putting others at ease with her ready smile and compassion.

She's one of the few people on the planet that takes my Father's preaching to heart and tries to live a pure and honest life. Father and Mother have been after me to marry, but even they admit that finding a virtuous woman in these troubled times is like trying to find a fist-sized ruby. Egyptus isn't just a ruby, she's a sparkling diamond. Or maybe a beautiful twinkling star, forever out of reach.

Egyptus stops in front of me. She's a sun-star today. Her long yellow dress peeks out from beneath her coat and gleams against her throat. I can't stop gazing into her eyes; they're so pure, such a beautiful brown, almost black, with thick lashes that sweep down when she has a shy or coy moment.

Thor interrupts this moment with a whinny. I clear my throat, handing her Night's reins. Our hands touch. I take hold of her fingers. Her dark skin is so smooth, so warm. It sends a tingle of pleasure through my body. We both laugh a little nervously and I say, "I guess we'd better head into town. Father should be getting there by now."

Egyptus nods. "Once word spreads that he's there, everyone will show up. He always has the best variety of goods, and at the best prices."

"That's how we keep business coming in."

I lean down and cup my hands together to boost her up. Egyptus places a boot in them. I admire her shapely lower limbs encased in green leggings as she springs onto Night's back. He turns his head and rolls a big eye back to look at her as she takes the reins, but he's well trained and otherwise doesn't move. They are a good pair -- the princess and the steed: both tall, dark, gentle, reliable.

Egyptus smiles down at me and I leap up behind her, straddling the horse. Wow. Her back is against my chest. We are so close. She's warm. I put my arms around her. This is pleasant beyond all description. She looks and smells like flowers and sunshine. I can't think, only breathe and feel.

My heart is pounding again. I feel Egyptus' heart throbbing too. Then Night is moving down the path and the rest of the horses tag along. Egyptus guides us through the palace's sunny vineyards and orchards. The whole world looks happy.

We make our way slowly through a meadow where the royal flock is grazing. Everything is beautiful. Perfect.

EGYPTUS: I still can't believe it. Ham's arms are around me. His warm, strong chest and broad shoulders are eased up against my back; his lean muscular arms are firmly around my torso, crossing under my chest. His thighs are snug behind mine as we straddle the bareback beast. He bends down to inhale the scent of my neck and I hear him groan then murmur, "Delicious."

My face is beginning to hurt, I am smiling so much. I feel like I felt in the dream with my mother last night --

safe and belonging. I feel like he's proud to be with me, like being together makes him happy.

The closer we get to town, the slower I lead the horses.

HAM: We leisurely pass through the village of Enoch to the market square, which is alongside the Silver River. This little city isn't named after *my* great-grandfather Enoch. This is a more ancient town founded by Adam's son Cain, and named by Cain after *his* son Enoch.

The city's stone houses are mostly low and ancient. But surrounding the market square they rise to two stories, with balconies from which to observe the happenings below: because generally, if anything at all is going to happen in this relatively out-of-the-way place, it will happen right here in the square.

A few small boats are moored on the sparkling river. Buyers and sellers are coming from the outlying areas and filling the colorful plaza, drawn by the fair weather and the prospect of a good trade.

My Father's arrival has greatly increased the market's size. The twelve servants we brought on this trip are efficiently unloading the horses and mules and spreading out mats to display our goods. Customers are flocking to them before things can be completely laid out. It looks like a long morning of trading.

Each of our servants is responsible for making the best deals possible. At the end of this expedition, when we return home to the Cainan valley, the profits will be totaled and split. Half will go to our family to support our ship-building enterprise and daily needs. The other half will be equally divided among the expedition's servants. This way they cooperate and actively protect our goods. In a good trading year they can become quite wealthy.

Egyptus halts Midnight by Father's stall. Already a few men are heading over to examine the small herd of spectacular horses trailing behind us. I slide off Night's back then turn to help Egyptus, holding her by the waist as she hops down and lands in front of me. We stand and look at each other. My hands don't want to leave her.

We reluctantly break our gaze as two of the palace servants catch up to accompany her at the market. I state the obvious: "I guess I'd better go show my horses, or the ones I have left."

Catching Midnight's reigns, I place them in her hand again. "After market, let's ride across the meadows and prove Night's worth the price."

She smiles. "I'll be back in a couple of hours."

I watch her as she walks away. She's even radiantly beautiful from the back.

Few men can afford one of my steeds, but they all want a look. Only Royalty and the richest of people throughout the world ride Thor's foals. Jarom, one of our servants, comes over to help me show them. In the end I sell one to Egyptus' uncle Mesael, her father's brother. He is a handsome man of average size. Charming and outgoing, he has as many small businesses as he does wives. He has a hard time parting with the gold required, but his pride requires that he ride the best horse possible.

He does look impressive cantering away on Firelight, the tall, noble, reddish-brown charger. I sigh. Another equine friend gone. The gold in my hand consoles me. We should be able to put the finishing touches on our ship this year.

I notice Egyptus talking to my Father. Two servants are standing behind her at a distance, one holding Night's reins, the other discreetly in charge of a small moneybag and a number of packages destined for the palace.

I smile. If only I could take her home with me. She could run my world so much more efficiently than I do. Just watching her converse with my Father brings me joy. Being on the same planet as her brings me joy.

EGYPTUS: I'm worried. Ham's father Noah says the ship is almost finished. "You should see it," he says, "it's taken us seventy years to build the huge Ark, but it's almost done. We'll finish installing stalls and partitions for the animals this summer and load it with supplies, then it will be ready. You need to find a way to join us, my child. Come before the rain does."

I hesitate, not wanting to give him false hope, or get my own hopes up. "I don't know if I'll be able to. You know how possessive my father is."

Noah gazes at me for a minute, seeming deep in thought. "Egyptus, I don't think the world has much longer. Look around the square." I look around and see people going about their business, the same as any other day, except Ham is here of course, gorgeous as ever.

"Egyptus." I return my attention to Noah. "You are one of the few, very few, who believe my message. The others," he waves his hand at the square, "they come listen because it's entertainment, but you come because you believe. You know what's going to happen, don't you?"

I nod. God is displeased. Everyone is going to die. I don't like to think about it.

Noah says, "Watch for the sign. Animals will head to our Cainan valley. They will come from all directions, including through this valley. Strange animals, ones you've never seen before. You must follow with them. If you wait until the rain becomes a downpour it will be too late."

I stare at the ground and sense tears coming. I feel what he says is true. "What if I can't come?" I whisper.

"If it is your desire to come, have faith that God will prepare a way for you." We are quiet for a minute. Noah sighs. "Egyptus, look at Ham." I wipe my moist eyes with the back of my hand then gladly look at my beloved Ham.

"My son has no wife. We are not poor, but for the last decades our money has been invested in the ship. What's left is in our trading goods. Because my preaching is considered an embarrassment, no girl is willing to marry Ham. No father wants to unite his family with ours."

I look at Noah. I hadn't thought about Ham's situation like this. Ham is so noble, so fine in every way, who wouldn't want him?

Noah continues, "None of this matters to Ham. His heart lives with you. Your unborn children need you to make it to the Ark."

I nod. Now I'm really crying. I wipe my eyes. Noah bends down, then straightens and hands me a lovely red and gold scarf from the trading goods piled beside him. I take it with a little choked laugh and dry my eyes and face.

I look at Noah, who is gazing at me with concern. I hesitate, then say what is too awful to be said: "I'm going to lose everything I have."

Noah looks about the square, then past it across the river to the valley around us. He sighs again then nods. "Yes, all this will be destroyed, but you will have Ham, and us, and your life. We will all have a new adventure together."

I smile a little at this and reply with resolve, "I will come. Somehow I will come. Not yet though. If I left now, papa would find me and bring me back."

Noah nods. "I trust your judgement. I will pray for you every day. Ham already does."

"And I for him," I reply.

Chapter Two

HAM: Leaving the six unsold stallions with Father and the servants, Egyptus and I ride Night and Thor out of the village of Enoch. Galloping, we leave the hamlet far behind in the valley until the horses slow on the mountain foothills. The sky continues bright blue, and the air is fresh and clear as we canter along. I want to comment on its beauty to Egyptus, but she is quiet and seems deep in thought.

We cover a good distance before I pull Thor alongside Midnight and we slow to a walk. I look at the expanse below us -- green and brown fields, winding Silver River, tiny trees, distant hazy mountains across the valley. Spring is exploding. The air is still cool. Egyptus is still quiet.

"I like your earrings," I say.

"They were my mother's."

"Yes, I know. Shem made them. My Mother gave them to her on the day you were born."

Amazed, Egypt touches a hand to an earring. "I didn't know that's where they came from. She wore these often."

"Yes, I saw her wear them to market a few times. I remember you with her too, when you were old enough to accompany her. You always stayed near her, often holding her hand."

"How strange you should tell me that memory. I dreamed about her and the market last night. I miss her so." She pulls out a red cloth embroidered with gold roses around the edge to dab at her eyes. She was crying earlier when talking to Father in the square, where I'd seen him hand her the scarlet scarf. Egypt probably doesn't realize that my sister-in-law Roseta wove and embroidered it.

I look away from her at the scenery, and give her a moment as the horses amble along. Clouds billow slowly across the blue sky, casting shadows on the fields in the valley below us.

Finally Egypt looks at me. I ask, "You okay?"

"No. Your father says the Ark is close to done. How can no one believe him?"

"Your mother did."

"Yes, she would have found a way to be on that ship. She did everything she could to be obedient to God."

"You do too."

"I try. I'm not as good as her, though."

"She'd had more practice. After all, you're only a half-century old. People don't seem to really start figuring themselves out and discovering their talents until around that age. I didn't start playing the lute until about then."

Egyptus smiles then says teasingly, "No wonder you're so good. You've had *so many* years to practice."

I smile her jab at my age. Really, no one expects a man to think about settling down until he's at least a century old, sometimes two or three. When you're going to live eight or nine centuries, it doesn't really matter. I shake my head at her in mock disgust. "I don't have my lute, or I'd play for you now and demonstrate all the benefits of *years* of practice. I've a new song for you. I'll play it tonight."

"Will you have a lute on the ship? Will you play for me there, too?"

"You will be on board?"

"Of course. I'll find a way."

I take a deep breath and let it out. I hadn't realized how much I'd been worrying about her answer. Now the world feels right again. Working on the Ark year after year, I've always envisioned Egyptus being on it: first with her mother, then after she passed away, having Egyptus with me.

"Well, it is a big ship. I'm sure we'll find room for a lute or two."

"How big is it?"

"The Ark is as big as God's heart. There's plenty of room for all who would enter."

"Who is coming?"

"So far just Father and Mother, my brothers Shem and Japheth, and their wives Roseta and Zaira. None of my other, older brothers and sisters are believers, not even any of my nieces and nephews. They think we're crazy and have separated themselves from us."

"Your mom must be sad."

"Yes, like you she's starting to realize the reality of what's going to happen."

"My papa shelters me, but I hear of the evil things people do. There's scarcely a family intact now days."

"Yes, and wars are raging between kingdoms. We're going to have to be watchful on this trading trip. Though God protects us, Father thinks it will be our last excursion."

Egyptus shakes her head. "Why go if it's so dangerous?"

"He really wants to preach one last time to all of the people possible. Give them one final warning. It is a big ship, after all."

EGYPTUS: Ham and I slow the horses to a walk. There's never too much time, never enough time, when we are together.

"When do you leave?" I ask.

Reluctantly he says, "Tomorrow morning. Father's in a hurry to make the circuit and get back to working on the ship."

I try to smile, though I'm sad he's leaving so soon. "I guess the next time I'll see you will be on the Ark. I'll have to come at the last minute, or papa will follow me and bring me back."

"Just come over the mountain pass. On a clear day you can see the ship from there, it's so big. When you get to the valley floor, follow the wide Green River down to Lake Zion. That's where Enoch's city of Zion was. When the city was taken up to heaven, the river filled in the hole it left. We are right there building where the river joins the lake. Ride Midnight, he'll know the way home."

"I've never traveled from Nod."

"I'll try to come and fetch you if Father thinks the flood is close."

"That would be a relief. I don't want to travel alone." The sun is creeping lower in the sky. "I must get back to the palace to make sure that dinner is ready, then I can go hear Noah preach."

"Right. I need to collect the money for Midnight. I assume you approve the purchase?" Ham quirks an eyebrow at me.

"Of course. I love this horse! We'll race you back," I call.

We take off. Speeding across the grass on Night's back lifts my mood. I laugh as Ham and Thor pretend to lose the race to us. They both look terribly dejected as we arrive at the palace.

Ham takes the horses and walks them in the courtyard, cooling them down from our run. I go inside.

"Papa," I call. He's in the throne room, just finished with his day. The last petitioners and those on trial are leaving, or being led away. I wait until they're gone then go to pat papa's shoulder. He's always tired after judgement day.

"Long day?" I inquire.

"Yes, it seems cases are becoming more complex, more difficult for me to judge. Sometimes I think everyone involved is guilty. But enough of that. How is the new horse? Did you have a good day?"

"Yes, Midnight rides like a dream. He's so well trained."

"So Ham is here for the payment?"

"He's in the courtyard."

"He didn't kiss you or anything, did he?"

I feel myself blush. "No, none of that."

"Good. I don't want you getting any ideas in your head about that boy. I don't mind you being his friend, and seeing him once or twice a year. Your mother was good friends with his family, particularly Annah, his mother, but I won't countenance anything more than that."

"I know papa." I look at the floor. I think papa believes that as long as I'm "infatuated" with a man I can't have, I'll be content to stay and run his house forever. Luckily he can't read my mind.

He seems to think it prudent to change the subject. "I'll send Irad out to pay Ham. I suppose you're going to the bonfire tonight?"

"Yes. Ham will escort me." Usually I go with a servant.

He gives me another probing look. "Don't be out late."

"I won't."

I kiss papa on top of his head then go to the kitchen with a big sigh of relief. I'm afraid that one of these days he'll cease to be so lenient about me spending time with Ham.

Adah the cook and one of her helpers are there. The food looks almost ready to serve. Early greens and radishes are laid out on a tray, glistening with oil and herbs. There are dark olives and colorful pickled preserves on another tray. Roasting game birds look golden and crispy and smell almost ready. A large river fish is prepared and set aside to fry at the last minute, and both light and dark wines sit ready to pour from carafes. Fresh raised buns are just coming out from the wood oven. They smell delicious. My stomach growls.

"Adah, everything looks perfect."

"And you look hungry. Take a bun."

"I'll take two, one for me and one for Ham."

"Sounds good."

"Maybe I'll take three buns. Two for me and one for Ham."

"Take four. Two apiece."

"It's a deal." I pile four hot golden buns in a clean cloth. "Thanks, Adah, and thank you for having everything ready."

"You're welcome, have fun."

I practically skip out of the kitchen and into the courtyard. Ham turns to me and I urge, "Let's get out of here before something happens to stop me."

Midnight has been paid for and taken to the stable, so Ham boosts me up on Thor and hops on behind. He reaches around and takes the reins, the warmth of his beloved embrace sending a shiver of pleasure through me. We are off to the city center -- and again, I can't stop smiling.

Chapter Three

HAM: It's almost sunset -- bonfire time. Egyptus and I leave Thor with the other horses at our camp just outside town, I grab my lute from our tent, and we walk into Enoch with Father. Wood and garbage has been stacked in the middle of the square, ready to be lit.

Father steps up on a platform at one end of the square so the rowdy crowd can see and hear him in the golden light. He's holding up my lute. "My friends," he calls. "My friends." The waiting crowd begins to settle.

They know this routine. We're not the only entertainment on the circuit. Musicians come through here, as well as storytellers. They are very popular. And troops of dancing girls, who are very popular indeed. However, we are the only entertainment this week.

"My friends, before the bonfire is lit, I will share with you a story."

The crowd is still distractedly finding places to sit and bundling up in blankets against the chilly air. The surrounding balconies are full. It looks like everyone in town has shown up tonight. There are families, couples, groups of friends; old and young toting their snacks and beverages and colorful blankets. Egyptus and I are sitting on the ground by the platform, sharing a blanket with red and blue stripes that I borrowed from our stash of trading goods.

Father continues, "But before my story, I present to you a great treat! Someone all of you have heard before." The crowd is starting to pay attention. "Someone who's music you love. The greatest musician in all the world -- my son Ham!" Applause erupts and I get to my feet and step onto the platform.

Father hands me my lute and I swing its strap over my head.

They need a lively song before I settle them down to listen to him. I raise my hands to speak. "All of you know that I love horses. How many of you love horses?" They roar their approval. "Here's a song about a little filly horse." I begin to strum and my lute emits a rhythm similar to a horse's trot. The audience claps along with the beat.

"I saw a little filly down by the stream.
I asked myself, now is she tame?
She looked at me and flicked her tail,

Then took off right on down the trail!

"Oh little filly filly come to me.
Oh little filly filly so pretty!"

A few of the smaller children are dancing to the beat.

"I saw a little filly under a tree.
I asked myself is she hungry?
I climbed the tree and tossed fruit down.
She ate the apples right from the ground.

"Oh little filly filly come to me.
Oh little filly filly so pretty!"

The audience has learned the chorus and is joining in.
The lute canters.

"I saw a little filly out in the rain.
To see her wet was such a shame.
I opened my pen and called, "come in."
She turned and ran as fast as wind.

"Oh little filly filly come to me.
Oh little filly filly so pretty!"

The audience out-sings me on that chorus. The lute gallops.

"I saw a little filly just run on by.
I wish I could race right by her side.
If I were a stallion fast and true,
Then I'd run faster and she'd pursue!

"Oh little filly filly come to me.
Oh little filly filly so pretty!"

We are all cheering together as the lute gambols to a stop.

I catch my breath. Now they need something calmer to prepare them for Father's sermon.

"Thank you, my friends," I call out. Raising my arms up, I take a big bow. The crowd cheers. "This next song is for all of us who haven't found our true love yet." I strum a chord. "How many of you are lonely tonight?" They laugh. No one wants to admit it. I begin plucking the tune: simple enough to remember, complex enough to enjoy.

"This is called 'A Sonnet to my Unmet Love.' Maybe it's for one of you beautiful women out there." There is a bit of feminine laughter. I glance at Egyptus and launch in with the words of the plaintive tune.

"If you do not exist, why are you missed?
My poor heart searches for you every day.
To gaze upon you face is what I've wished.
I try to tell myself it is okay.

"But it is not, I can't deny that now.
I'm weary waiting for your appearance.
I've waited and I've searched and now I vow
To soon grow accustomed to your absence.

"But I cannot be reconciled to this,
Your place within my heart remains unfilled.
My every cell throbs deep with loneliness.
Only by your sweet balm will I be healed.

"I doubt my judgement, though I've felt from birth,
That you are walking somewhere on this earth."

I repeat the tune on the lute, making it fancier, more intense with longing, then sing the chorus again looking down into Egyptus' eyes:

"I doubt my judgement, though I've felt from birth,
That you are walking somewhere on this earth."

I finish with a slow chord.

The crowd pauses, then claps loudly. I bow my thanks.

"Thank you all. Now here is the great and wonderful Noah, who is here for your listening pleasure with a classic story." Father comes to stand beside me. I bow to him then hop from the platform to sit by Egyptus, with my lute swung on its strap over my back. She gives me a sweet smile then a little pat on the shoulder, as if to say *good job*.

Mission accomplished. I live to please her.

Father is dressed for the stage with a blue turban on his whitening hair, and a long blue and gold robe with flowing sleeves that fall and flutter as he lifts his arms and gestures. It's quite theatrical.

The last glow of the sun is fading as he begins, "My people, my friends. You have heard that I have built a large ship. I invite you all to come and see it. I will show you the beauty of its design, for God has had it built to save his believing children."

A large man pipes up, "What if we all can't fit inside?"

He replies, "Then that means there are enough righteous people to save the world. God will hold back the rain and flood." There are a few skeptical snorts from the audience.

Father's tough. He hasn't been preaching for five hundred years for nothing. He practically thrives on heckling.

"Your God – the Father of your spirits – loves you. He wants you to be happy. That is why He has given you commandments." More snorts, a few guffaws.

Father continues, "Think about it, who can be happy when they are hurting another, when their family is falling apart, or they feel guilty because they have cheated, or stolen, or lied? No one can have peace in their heart when they know that their actions bring distress and contention to themselves and others."

The audience is truly uncomfortable now, starting to clamor. Soon they'll be throwing things.

Father waits for them to calm. Then he begins again.

"Our first parent, Adam, lived long ago in a beautiful garden. He was perfect: strong and handsome and good. And he was lonely." Father gestures to a family sitting in the front and asks, "Children, how you would feel if you had no one to play with?"

"Bored," the oldest boy replies.

Father asks the mother, "Madam, how would it be to have no one to talk to?"

"Sad," she says.

He directs himself to the father of the young family. "Sir, how lonely are we men when there's no one to smile and share with?"

The husband looks over at his wife. "Very lonely."

The audience relaxes. They like a good story and they know this one. "So God gave Adam a wife. Do you know her name?"

"Eve," a young girl calls out with a nervous giggle.

"That's right: 'Eve.' They obeyed all of God's commandments. He visited them and they were truly happy. Then do you know what happened?"

"The apple," a low voice states from the back of the crowd.

"That's right," Father continues, "Eve listened to Satan, who also walked in the Garden. He told her she could have more knowledge if she ate fruit from The Tree of Knowledge of Good and Evil, even though God had said that she and Adam weren't to partake of it. Eating it turned her mortal. That means her body would get old and someday die. It was the first time anyone had ever disobeyed God on this earth.

"Adam ate it too because he knew she'd be sent out of the Garden for being disobedient, and he wanted to stay with Eve, his wife and best friend.

So God made them both leave the Garden. Do you know why?"

There's a pause, then Egyptus speaks up, "The other apple."

"Right," Father says. "There was another tree: The Tree of Life. If they ate its fruit they would turn immortal again and live forever."

Father asks all of us, "So why didn't God just solve the problem by letting Adam and Eve stay and eat the fruit of the Tree of Life? They could have gone on living in the Garden forever."

The listeners are truly puzzled by this question.

Finally I call out, "Sin."

"Right," Father says. "Sin. They had been disobedient by eating the apple, and no unclean person can be in God's presence unless the mortal Messiah pays for their sin. They needed to leave the Garden of Eden so that they could repent as mortals, and become clean again.

"So they left and began having children. Their children also sinned. The family grew and split into tribes and now we have our separate kingdoms."

Father asks a final question: "So is there hope for us to live with God someday?"

The audience is quiet. After a pause a wizened voice in the middle of the crowd calls out, "Yes there is!"

Father peers at the tiny old man bundled up in a sheepskin. He smiles and nods. "Thank you, sir. You are correct. Because we are mortal we can repent of our mistakes, ask God for forgiveness, and do our best to follow His commandments with love and peace in our hearts. If we do this, someday through God's plan a Messiah will pay for our sins, and we will be resurrected and live with Him again."

The crowd has had enough preaching. Father gives his final push: "Leave your sins behind. Come to the Ark when you see groups of animals headed for its shelter. You will survive the coming flood."

The message was short, but not sweet to the listeners. The bonfire is lit as they turn to their revels.

Father's shoulders slump. He looks out over the carousing public. "Goodbye. Goodbye my friends."

Egyptus and I stand and join him as he steps off the platform. Father doesn't look back as I put an arm around his shoulders to comfort him. We leave the square, walking through the dark city, leaving the firelight and the noisy crowd behind.

Chapter Four

NEHOR: We've had too much wine, but there will be more. A troop of "serving girls" has been brought in from outside the palace. They served our meal and are now mostly sitting on our laps, not very clothed, providing "entertainment."

The household servants and Egyptus know to avoid the dining room when my brothers come over for dinner. It's always an occasion.

Two tipsy girls with tambourines are singing and dancing together. One of the girls lunges too close to the wall, knocking one of the ancient urns off the shelf. I see it fall and break. It's a family heirloom. I'll worry about it later.

EGYPTUS: Ham reluctantly says, "I guess I'd better take you back."

We are sitting by the dying fire in the center of his camp, sharing the striped blanket. I murmur, "I don't want to go home. I know what's going on there."

"I'll tell you what, first I'll sing you your song, then I'll wake up Thor and take you home."

"I thought you already sang my song in the square."

"Nope, there's another just for you."

Standing, he goes into the tent he shares with his father and reappears with the lute, then comes and sits cross-legged facing me. The half moon is up, but even with the glowing coals from the fading fire there's not much light.

He strokes each string, making sure they're in tune and makes a minor adjustment to one of them.

The first notes of my song burst out in the crisp air, rippling out across the tents and fields, expanding into the twinkling universe above us. There's a pause. For a moment I feel like all creation is anticipating Ham's gift of music.

"Egyptus," he says in a low voice, "before I begin, I just want to let you know that I have a very active imagination. Especially when it comes to you."

I blush in the dark. He plucks the strings and sings:

"Yours has become such a beloved face,
I feel as your cheek rests against my chest.
Contentment is complete in your embrace.
Upon you I am fixed, I love you best.

"My cells are all alive within your arms.
Our souls are matched and closely do commune.
Amazement passes through, and my heart warms,
That you and God have granted me this boon.

"I tilt my head and look into your eyes.
Their warmth and love amazes me still yet.
Infused with bliss that no rhyme close describes.
Sensation hums unvoiced in me, secret.

"Enfolded by you is my favorite place.
Yours has become such a beloved face."

The notes slow. Finally the last one drifts out to the mountains and stars. Silence.

I sniff. Oh dear, I'm crying again.

Ham stands up and heads to his tent. I wipe my eyes with the red scarf. He returns luteless and extends a warm hand to help me to my feet.

With his arm around my waist, we walk past the tents to where the horses are congregated. He whistles a different whistle and only Thor comes trotting to stand beside us.

Ham turns to me but instead of boosting me up, his arms go around me. He pulls me against his body. Heaven. I tilt my head up and his lips are on mine. Oh new, sweet, strange sensation. My body is turning to liquid. Let this last forever.

Ham lifts his head, then lowers his lips to mine again, for longer this time. His hand strokes my back. I feel my knees weakening. My arms are around him. No wonder Adam left the garden with Eve. They had obviously discovered kissing.

Ham finally breaks our bond. He's breathing deeply. "Wow..." he mumbles. "I guess my imagination wasn't nearly as good as I thought." I melt in his embrace, my cheek on his chest, feeling cherished to my bones. We cling together, the heavens turning above us.

Finally I speak. "I love you too. I noticed that bit in your song."

Ham lifts his chin and rests it on top of my head. "Yes, I love you. Of course I do. I always have."

Eventually he pulls back and kisses my forehead. "I must get you back."

"Okay, not my first choice though."

"But practical."

"Yes, I don't want to upset papa. Once before I was born, a band of men took my mother, intending to ransom her back to papa. He tracked them down and killed them all. All ten of them. Single-handedly. No one ever bothered her again."

"I remember hearing about that when it happened. I heard there were twenty he killed."

"No. Only ten."

"Still, I'd better take you back."

"He's probably still carousing with my uncles. I'll go in through the kitchen."

Ham squeezes me to him. "Please, please make it to the Ark."

"Your father says God will help me."

"Then we'll have faith."

We arrive at the palace too soon, pausing outside the gate, not wanting Thor's hooves clattering on the courtyard cobblestones calling attention to our arrival. We don't dismount. Ham's arms are still around me, his breath at the back of my neck. He traces kisses along its base, sending a shiver through me.

Finally he jumps down, then pulls me off the horse tightly into his arms. He kisses me hard, desperately. I return kiss for kiss, knowing this is the last batch of kisses for now, and maybe forever.

Finally we part and I turn to go through the portals, our hands still clinging. We don't want to hear the word *goodbye*, so we don't say anything. My hand slips from his as I pass through the gate.

'Don't cry,' I tell myself.

There's a lantern burning by the front door, where the palace guard is on duty, but I wave to him as he comes to close the gate behind me, and I head to the side of the house.

'Don't cry.' I find the kitchen door and slip through, shutting it quietly behind me. 'Don't cry. Don't cry. Get to your room, then you can cry. Alone.'

Passing into the unlit hallway, I hear male voices. I slip past the dining room, then hear my name. My papa and uncles are talking about me. It's unusually quiet. Where are the dancing girls? Where's the carousing?

NEHOR: Mesael, Nabal, and I are bent over the map in the middle of the table. The ancient map. The one passed down from our second father Cain. The one hidden all these years in the now broken urn.

We've identified our valley on it. It seems to have been drawn before our tribe settled it. There are the other valleys and plains which now have their kingdoms.

And there on the west side of the map is the Garden of Eden. Yes, the actual Garden. With instructions detailing how to enter, and how to identify the Tree of Life. Oh yes. If this is real, and if the Garden and Tree are still there, we have it made. Eternal life, here we come.

Nabal points to Eden on the map. "According to this, it would take at least a month to get to the Garden. Probably much longer. Then we'd have to return. Can you really leave your kingdom that long? Egyptus has never been in charge for such a long time before, and you haven't exactly let any of your other children run anything."

"I don't trust them," I reply. "And besides, I'm planning on running things for two or three hundred more years. I'm not that old."

"True," Nabal states. "Father would still be running things if we hadn't conveniently involved him in the 'skirmish' with the 'bandits'."

"I guess that's why I don't trust my own children. Look what we did to poor papa. If we come back immortal from Eden, I'll run this place for millennia."

Mesael says, "Oh surely you'll get bored with being the king after a few more centuries. There's so much more to enjoy in life."

I snort, "Spoken like a man with seven wives."

"As far as I'm concerned, I can never have enough women."

"Once again, no, you are not adding Egyptus to your collection."

"But what if we're immortal? I'd give all the rest away and have only her for her lifetime. After that, of course, I'd be business as usual."

I sigh. Mesael is incorrigible. He's the youngest of us three. Well built, his good looks certainly help him practice his favorite 'hobby'."

Nabal says, "We don't even know if Eden's still there, or if it is, if the Tree is still there. It would be a huge gamble to go. We could all lose everything in the time we are gone."

Nabal is incessantly thinking. He's the most calculating of us three. Short, sturdy, and clever, he's not the richest for nothing. Being the king, I should be the wealthiest, but I'm not. I enjoy the power, but leave the kingdom's finances to my brother. The three of us formed a bond at papa's death and have kept that secret and many others. Together, if we live long enough, we will take over the world. Everything on this map will be ours.

We contemplate the map. Finally Nabal points to the kingdoms to our west. "We have been waiting for Sharon to invade Havilah. We know that is now happening. Once that war is over, our plan is to take them both over while they are still weakened."

Mesael and I nod. Nabal continues, "That means that we will be at war this fall, or at the latest, next spring. We would have plenty of time to go to Eden and back, collect the army, and attack. On the other hand, if we return from our trip immortal, it will certainly be easy to take over all the kingdoms, one after another. If only we could be sure the Garden's still there, although these instructions on how to enter and which fruit to eat are really clear, so I think that there's a good chance it is."

I say, "Yes, otherwise why would there be a map? What if just one of us goes? One could bring back fruit for the other two."

Mesael looks at me doubtfully. "Could you really resist taking immortality for yourself alone? I don't think I could. It's the three of us or none of us. That's the way it's always been."

"Mesael's right," Nabal says. "Too tempting. If we fight among ourselves, we really will lose everything."

I ask, "So should we go?"

"It's probably worth the risk," Nabal replies. "If it's not there, we'll lose some time, and perhaps some possessions, but we'd find a way to get them back. If it's there, we gain everything."

"I'm in," Mesael says. "Eternity is not long enough to do all the things, and all the women, I want to."

"Okay," I say.

Mesael is enthusiastic. "A trip will be fun, and a great story later."

EGYPTUS: I've heard enough. I'm so tired. Surely this is just a bad dream -- a hallucination. I slip down the hallway to my room so silently, I'm afraid to even breathe. Luckily the door is open enough for me to slip inside. The hinges would squeak.

I go in and take off my outer clothes and lie on my bed. Everything is swirling in my brain: Ham, the Ark, Eden, papa, marriage, kisses, murder. It's too much. I'm too exhausted to cry or sort through anything. I fall asleep — or pass out. I don't know which.

Chapter Five

EGYPTUS: I don't sleep well and wake up before the first hint of light. Realization hits. This is not good. I think it really happened. The best day of my life, ruined by eavesdropping on three murderers. And one of them is my father. This really isn't good. Maybe it wasn't real.

I roll over and sit up. I'd better find out. I climb out of bed, put on the same clothes I had on yesterday, quickly wash my face, and pull my hair back. I can hear Adah in the kitchen as I head to the dining room and light a candle.

The room is a mess. The table's been cleared off, but there are dishes and platters stacked on the sideboard, and a broken urn on the floor. Wait a minute. That's the Kings' Urn -- passed down from one ruler to another. Now it's in pieces. And empty. It must have held the map they were looking at. It wasn't a dream. Horrors. They might head to Eden. Worse, they might become immortal and become unstoppable. Worse yet, papa might give me to uncle Mesael as a wife.

I go over to the broken Urn. I've never held it before, but now I pick up the three large pieces it broke into. They're made of thick clay with a dark blue glaze, and are relatively heavy. The lid is lying face down beside it.

I carry the pieces and lid down the hall to my room and set them on the sideboard under the metal mirror on the wall. Piecing the urn together, I hold it there with my hands, then take it apart again.

There's an inscription inside the lid. It's written in Adamic, the language that all tribes have spoken since Adam.

Luckily, I read and write. It says:

"Bow to me from the East
Wash before entering.
Ascend with a prayerful heart."

Enter. Ascend. This must be a clue on how to enter the Garden. Hopefully, if this was left cast on the floor, papa didn't read it. The fewer clues he has, the better. I take the lid and put it in the chest with my clothes.

To my surprise, papa is standing in the dining room when I return. Why is he up so early?

"Papa!" I say cheerfully, trying to act unsuspicious. "Did you have a good night?"

"Yes, did you?"

"Yes, Ham sang. Noah preached. Repentance. Ark. Same as always. I was home before midnight."

"Good." He sits down wearily at the table.

"I'll go see what's for breakfast." I head to the kitchen.

"Yes, I need my tea."

I return with steeped tea, fill his cup, then add a touch of honey. Adah comes in behind me with fresh buns, cheeses, and scrambled eggs. The nourishment should help papa's tummy and head. He always has too much wine when the uncles come.

We eat in silence. I find I'm hungry despite my trepidation, and eat twice as much as usual. I didn't eat a lot yesterday. Papa eats half as much as usual, but the color starts returning to his face. After three cups of hot tea, he pushes his plate aside.

"Egyptus, I'm going to have to leave you in charge of the household. I'm going on a journey with my brothers."

Oh no. This is very bad.

I feign surprise. "Really? Where are you going?"

"The tribes to the west are at war. We're going to see if we can negotiate an agreement between them, a treaty."

Liar. Liar. Liar. "When will you leave?"

"The sooner the better. My brothers should be arriving in a few minutes."

"How long will you be gone?"

"We might be gone most of the summer, maybe less. I'm not certain."

I look troubled. "Oh papa, I've never been in charge for that long. Must you go? Couldn't you wait? Maybe the tribes will work it out on their own. Please wait until autumn at least."

"Egyptus, you can do this. You're fifty years old. Many girls your age are running their own households without their fathers. And besides, you're already in charge here."

That is true.

"Are you taking Ahab? Ham trained him well and he's used to your trips."

"Yes, Ahab and I are a good team."

"I really wish you wouldn't go." I rise and go around the table to give him a squeeze and kiss the top of his head. A murderer's head. What a shame.

I indicate the corner of the room, "Did you see that the King's Urn got broken?"

"Yes, I'm afraid there was an accident last night. Very unfortunate."

"Was it empty?"

"Yes. I was expecting ashes of ancestors or something dramatic after all these centuries. Very anticlimactic, really."

Liar. Liar. Liar.

"I took the pieces to my room."

"Whatever you want, my dear. I must finish packing now."

After he leaves I sit at the table, my forehead in my hands. Disbelief wars with devastation. He's really going to Eden. Crazy old man.

NEHOR: Mounted on Ahab, I wave goodbye to Egyptus and the rest of the household standing on the porch. Egyptus looks rather forlorn standing there, waving farewell in the early light. She's trying to be brave, but her eyes are full of tears. She looks so worried that I almost jump off Ahab so that I can give her a hug and tell her; "Of course I'm not going to leave you to go find the Garden of Eden and become immortal. I'll just stay here."

But I don't. She'll be fine. It's not like I'll never see her again.

Chapter Six

EGYPTUS: It's chilly outside, but I don't go back in for my coat. I need advice and must get to Noah's camp before they leave. I head around to the stable, a low, longish building behind the house. The door creaks as I open it. Midnight is in the third stall down. He comes over to greet me.

"Let's go find your daddy," I whisper. He lets me put on his bridle. I lead him outside then climb up the mounting block and onto his back. Other than Thor, he's probably the tallest horse I've ever been on. We head around the house and through the courtyard. Jael is on guard this morning. Tall and straight, he hurries from his post by the door and opens the gate for me.

"Good morning, Jael."

"Good morning, Miss."

I go through the gate and he shuts it behind me.

Night seems to know where I want to go, and we speed toward Noah's camp. I begin to shiver both from the cold and my fraying nerves. Gold and pink are streaking the sky in front of us as we head east. Midnight emits crisp puffs of steam as he breathes. Everything is fresh and dewy, smelling like new earth and green growth. It really is a perfect morning, despite the chill. Too bad my life is falling apart.

Noah's camp is busy. Two of the three tents are down. The efficient crew is loading merchandise on the animals. I need Ham. I need him to hug me and to feel his warmth and strength infuse into me.

Oh no! I'm too late. His horses aren't in the field. I want to cry.

Midnight and I pull up in the middle of what's left of the camp and Kahleel, the head servant, runs over.

"Is Ham gone?"

"Yes Egyptus, he left a little while ago to get a head start with his horses and our slower mules. Noah's in his tent, though." I look at the remaining soft oiled-leather tent. It's not terribly big, as it has to be packed and carried long distances, but there is plenty of room for two tall men to stand, move around, and sleep.

"Will you help me down, please?" Kahleel helps me off Midnight, though not as smoothly as Ham does. I want Ham.

"May I come in?" I ask at the entry to the tent. Noah's head appears between the flaps.

"Egyptus, come in!" I pass through the tent flap. "Have you changed your mind? Can you come with us now?"

Overwhelmed, I sit down on a stool without being invited. Tears start rolling down my cheeks.

"Oh, my dear," Noah says in a fatherly way. He comes over to put his arm around my shoulders. "You're so cold!" he says upon touching me.

Soon he's pulled a thick dark blue coat around my shoulders. It smells like wool and Ham. He drags up a stool and sits facing me. I reach under the coat into my yellow dress pocket and pull out the red cloth he gave me yesterday and start wiping my eyes and nose. Looking up at him, I give a watery laugh.

"I've sure got a lot of use out of your gift," I say, indicating the scarf.

"Glad to be of service." Noah grins back. Today he's dressed in a knee-length dark grey tunic and leggings, with a brown belt and boots. His greying hair is swept back from his face, and his beard neatly trimmed. How like Ham he is. I feel a little comforted.

"What is bothering you, my dear? Were you just hoping to see Ham?"

Yes. No. "Oh Noah." I begin to cry again and in between sobbing breaths I tell him the horrible truth – that I overheard papa reveal that he and my uncles murdered their father, and that they found the map of Eden and are intending to become immortal and terrorize the world. I leave out the part about becoming Mesael's wife. I'll die before I let that happen.

My sobs subside as the story ends. Finally there's just a few hiccups left.

Noah is quiet, watching me. He begins to pat my hand. "No wonder you're upset."

I take a few deep breaths to calm myself, then ask, "Do you think Eden's still there?"

"I'm not sure. It's been two thousand years since God set guards around it to keep Adam and Eve out, but they knew where it was and how to enter. Their children might have known too, at least the older ones. Probably their son Cain drew that map, if it's been passed down in your family. Anyway, the whole face of the land will be changed by the flood, so if Eden's there now, it will soon be washed away."

I lament, "Oh, why did they have to find that map now? If the guards have left and they get inside and eat the fruit of the Tree of Life, won't they survive the flood?"

"Yes they would."

"Papa and his brothers would be dreadful as immortals. I have to stop them. I'll follow them. Somehow, if they succeed, I'll trick them into eating the fruit of the Tree of Knowledge and turn them mortal again."

Now Noah looks worried. "That's a lot for you to take on, my dear. If it's there, I can't imagine God would leave it unguarded."

I take a deep breath. "I heard them say that the map has instructions on it. If there's a way to get in and pass by the guards, they will. If only I'd seen the map myself I could get there without having to follow them."

"I know where Eden is."

I am astounded. "You do?"

"Sure. It's not that hard to find. My sons were born near there."

"You mean Ham was born near the Garden of Eden?"

"Yes, I mean Shem, Ham, and Japheth. Annah and I had many children before those three, but they all got caught up in the world's wickedness. My wife and I were very discouraged. Here I was preaching to the world, and not even my own children would listen. So we decided to try again.

"We moved west and built up a little farm in a deserted area, right near the Mountain of Eden. The whole of Eden Valley and Plain is considered cursed by the surrounding tribes, so we were left alone. Annah gave birth to the three boys after I was five hundred years old. We raised them on scriptures and hard work.

"The boys had the run of the valley. They played in the forest, became great swimmers in the lake, learned to make and build everything -- from tools, to furniture, to clothing. Very handy skills to use later for Ark-building. It was a lot of fun really, just us five." Noah sits quietly reminiscing for a few seconds.

I say, "I didn't know any of this about Ham. No wonder he acts so differently from other males. He grew up in a different world."

"Yes, plus basically he's a very good man. That's where he started to care for horses. He always had a knack with animals. Even the wildest ones seem tame around him."

Noah continues, "Finally when the boys were in their twenties, we had a family discussion. Every fall we'd all go into civilization to trade our goods for supplies. The wilderness giants had attacked and tried to kill us that year near their territory, when we were on our way to Hannanihah to trade.

"Also, by then we knew that the flood was coming. The world had really deteriorated just in the time we'd been away.

"We decided to move back to the Cainan valley and begin building the Ark. I would resume my trading business and preach again, trying to save as many souls as I could. The boys would find wives.

"So we packed up and came back. Ham brought Thor with him, along with his other horses. He always said Thor was one of the original animals from the Garden of Eden. I'm beginning to believe it. He's really old for a horse, but seems young. Anyway, yes, I know where the Garden is."

Noah has just boggled my mind.

My musings are interrupted by a voice outside the tent: "Noah? We're packed up. Are you ready for us to take your tent down?"

Noah rises, walks to the tent flap, and opens it. "I'll be a bit longer, Kahleel. Egyptus needs some counseling, then we'll be on our way." He finds parchment and charcoal and returns to sit in front of me.

"Now, let me draw you a map. The land of Eden is relatively easy to find. You see, all four of the major rivers have their genesis in the Garden of Eden. So, you'll just need to follow the Pison River, which flows through this land of Nod, to its source.

"See, here is the Pison River, you call it the Silver River." He indicates it on the map he's creating. "Follow it up through the mountain pass into the land of Sharon, then the land of Havilah.

"Keep following it. You'll go through a wilderness of misty hills where the giants live. They are friends with your tribe, so should let you pass through their territory. They won't follow you into the land of Eden though. Their superstition says that no giant ever returns from there.

"Then you'll be on Eden Plain. Keep following the river. It will lead you to Eden Valley, where there's a mountain with four sides. The Garden is on the top of the mountain. It's too steep to climb, so you'll have to find the entrance. It's hidden, of course."

"You've no idea where the entrance is?"

"No, sorry."

He continues drawing. "I am going the opposite way: east to Heni. Then we'll trade in the northern lands of Omner, Enoch, and Shum before circling south again through Nod and back to Cainan."

I examine the map he's drawn me while talking. "I think I can follow this."

"Good girl. This isn't to scale, of course, but you'll get there. I'll catch up with Ham and send him back here to accompany you."

"No, please don't. I know papa would kill him if he found us together on the journey. He'd probably kill me too."

"Hmmm. I don't know if I can keep Ham from coming once I tell him about the map's discovery."

"Then don't tell him."

Noah gets up and begins pacing back and forth in the small tent.

"That's not fair. He'd want to help you, and you might need the help."

"Let's leave it up to fate. You can tell him once he sells the rest of his horses. He has six left. Maybe by then this problem will be solved. Let's see what happens."

Noah purses his lips then nods his head thoughtfully. "Agreed. Pack carefully. Think about what you'll need, how you'll get food and protect yourself."

"I'm tall, and strong. I think I'll disguise myself as a boy. I could probably take enough goods to look like a trader."

"You should probably avoid all humans possible, though that's hard to do, as they like to live along the river. Just go as a traveler, not a trader. I don't want you to be attacked by ruffians for your wares. The lands are at war now and can be lawless."

I sigh. "Okay. Will you do me a favor?" I remove my mother's earrings from my ears. I'd slept with them on. "Will you take these to the Ark for me? They were my mother's, and they're my favorite. I'd at least like to know that they're safe and that a part of her will survive the flood. Maybe that's silly, but it will give me comfort to think of it." I place the earrings in Noah's hand.

"Of course, my dear. They will be there waiting for you when you arrive."

"I'll try to make it, but I don't fear death. I know I'll be with God and that I'll see mother again. But I'd rather live and be with you and Ham for now."

Noah gives a little laugh. "You know, in all my years of preaching, I've heard many people say they believe my words and that they believe in God, but I think only a very few of you have actually had the courage and conviction to live what you believe."

I stand and give him a brief hug, then step back. "Thank you."

"Okay, my dear. Take the coat with you. It's cold and I'm sure Ham would want you to have it."

I smile and run my fingers down its front. "I'll wear it as part of my disguise."

Noah nods, then goes to open the tent flap. The servants and loaded horses are waiting. I pass through, then turn back. "Say 'hello' to your wife Annah for me."

"I will."

He follows me to Midnight, who is patiently standing where I left him. I say, "This is such a well-trained horse."

"Yes, he might be a good companion for a trip, though he's a bit ostentatious."

Night looks at Noah and snorts his disgust.

I grin. Noah cups his hands and boosts me onto Night's back, exactly as Ham does. "Take care. Go with God."

"You too."

I wave goodbye as Midnight turns and canters away. When I look back, Noah's tent is being taken down.

Chapter Seven

EGYPTUS: Early the next morning I enter the kitchen dressed in papa's clothes and a belt with a sheathed short sword, which I've also taken from papa's room. I pull Ham's coat on. The sleeves are long on me so I've rolled them up. I tie the belt closed, then sling a pack over my back. Adah looks me up and down. "Your sister won't know you, Miss."

"Zillah understands it's safer for me to travel as a boy. I expect to stay at her house for five nights, maybe six. Thanks for doing my hair yesterday."

"You're welcome, Miss."

It had taken hours for Adah's quick hands to braid my long hair into tiny rows. Between the masculine ponytail of tiny braids, my height, and angular features, I pass as a boy.

I check my chest. Suitably flat. Binding my breasts is much more comfortable for horseback riding. This isn't the first time I've bound my breasts before getting on a horse; just the first time I've added boy's clothes over them.

"You be careful."

"I will, Adah. You've always been so good to me, especially since mama died. I want you to know how much I appreciate you." Impulsively I give her a tight squeeze. Pleased, she hands me a sack filled with food.

"Do take care, Miss. Go with God."

"I will." We share a smile, then I step outside through the kitchen door.

I head to the stable and find Midnight waiting in his stall. He looks at me expectantly, not at all fooled by my disguise.

"Hey, Midnight, are you ready to go?" He nuzzles my head. I think he's starting to like me.

I put Night's harness strap around his chest and fasten it behind his neck at the base of his mane. Walking around to his chest, he nuzzles me again as I pass the T-strap, connected to the chest strap, between his forelegs. The other end of the t-strap is connected to the body strap that comes around the body behind the legs and fastens to the chest strap behind the neck.

This contraption is what most bareback horse riders use. It's lighter than a heavy saddle, allows the rider to secure belongings to the horse, and is a place to hang on when the horse is running. It's also convenient to connect a tether rope to. Ham invented this, and Thor has made it fashionable.

Night is used to his harness strap, which was included in his sale price. I slip a bridle around his head then pick up the sleeping roll that I've left in the stall, and lead him out of the stable.

"Bow." He obeys the command Ham taught him, and I climb on just behind his harness and slide back a few inches. Night stands up as soon as I'm on. I settle the sleeping roll and food sack in front of me, then tie them to the harness. We head around the house and Jael opens the gate for us.

"You're leaving on your journey, Miss."

"Yes, Jael. I'm headed for Zillah's."

"You're sure you don't want one of the guards to accompany you?"

"There's no need, it's just an hour across the river. If I follow the road, I'll be there before breakfast."

"Very good, Miss."

"Thank you, Jael. Thanks for everything."

Midnight and I go through the gate and turn west. We trot by the rock wall surrounding the palace, then through the orchard and out into the royal pasture with its cows and goats.

I stop Night, and turn to look at my home one last time. It's beautiful. I might never see it again. I'm numb inside. Maybe that's best for now.

The sky behind the palace is streaked with peach and purple. It's going to be a beautiful day for riding.

I turn back around and Midnight and I veer north through the green fields toward the river. Zillah is one of many children papa had with another wife who died before he married my mother. If I could convince another person to come on the Ark with me, I would choose Zillah, my favorite sister. But she's already told me she doesn't believe any of "Noah's nonsense," and won't come.

If I were going to her house, I would cross at the bridge and follow the northwest road. Zillah's community is one hour's journey toward Shum, the kingdom that is ruled by papa's Uncle Jubal.

But I am not going toward Shum. I'm headed west to Sharon.

Midnight and I reach the river. A well-worn road winds its way alongside. This is the trail Night and I will take, hopefully uninterrupted, until we reach Eden Mountain. I plan on catching up with papa's party and passing them at some point, arriving before them at Eden, and figuring out a way to prevent their immortality.

NEHOR: Nabal, Mesael, and I arrive at the mountain pass into Sharon. The Silver River runs down a narrow gorge that gouges through the mountain range dividing Sharon and Nod. The river is running high because it's spring, so we take the steep trail that has been cut out of the side of the crevasse.

When we invade Sharon we will come in the autumn when the river is at its lowest so that the army can ford directly up through the gorge. Or, we could march up through Shum then enter from the northeast.

I ruminate on the benefits of both invasion plans as I follow Mesael's horse over the trail, trying not to look down. One miss-step and Ahab and I will fall a great distance into the rushing water far below.

I'm thinking invading from Shum might be the better plan. Then we wouldn't have to worry about this ravine. I wonder if Uncle Jubal and his army would like to join the invasion, but then we'd have to split the spoils. Hmmm.

My musing is interrupted as the trail begins to drop and the vast plain of Sharon comes into view. It's marvelous -- so fertile. Filled with farms, orchards, patches of forest, and untilled land. Plenty of wealth here. I will enjoy ruling this forever.

The question is, should I let the current inhabitants stay, or wipe them out and re-settle the land with Caananites? Grandfather Lamech wiped out the existing population when he invaded Shum. I think about that as we descend to the valley floor and continue to follow the river.

EGYPTUS: It's getting dark. I am uneasy. Where do I stop for the night? Midnight and I have been going all day, passing small villages and other travelers. Fishermen. Children laughing and playing in the streams feeding the river. Women washing clothes.

I'm sore from riding. Hungry too. We stopped briefly at midday to stretch and rest. I ate one of last fall's stored apples and some of Adah's fresh buns, then it was back on Midnight. Riding all day is a lot different than riding for a few hours in the morning or afternoon. I feel so stiff. I'm not sure I can get off Night, much less walk. We need to stop.

I direct Night to a stand of trees. "Bow," I say and he does. Slowly and painfully I dismount. I can still stand. Barely.

Hobbling to the nearest tree, I take off Night's bridle and tether him by his harness, giving him lots of slack for grazing. He must be tired too. He begins chomping at the short tufts of new spring grass.

Actually, he looks perfectly happy. I guess horses are better travelers than palace princesses.

I roll out my bedroll just far enough away from him that he won't step on me, and ease myself down on it. It's getting really dark.

I pull fresh food from the sack: strawberries bundled in a cloth knotted closed at the top. A little smashed, but smelling of home. More buns. I'm getting homesick just from the taste.

Now it's dark. I can't see much, other than stars and silhouettes of trees and mountains. It's getting colder so I lay down and wrap the sheepskin bedroll around me. I hear the river and crickets. A distant wolf howls. What if it attacks in the night? What if someone finds and attacks me? What if someone steals my obviously expensive horse?

This is so stupid. Why did I think I could do this? 'Oh God, please watch over me and Midnight this night.'

I will turn around and go home in the morning. I'd go right now, but I'm too tired and sore to move out of this bedroll. I'm even too tired to cry.

Well, maybe not. There's one rogue tear trickling from the corner of my eye.

NEHOR: We've passed two villages and a larger town as we continue west into Sharon. The inhabitants are mostly women and children. The men have been ordered off to fight in the war with Havilah, leaving their homes unprotected -- easy prey for an invading army.

The villagers have been very willing to sell us food and drink. We have plenty of money to pay. There are even inns in the larger towns. With the failing light we are stopping at one now. This trip might not be so bad after all.

EGYPTUS: Midnight and I are still heading west. We've come a long way today. I can see a mountain range in the distance. When I woke up this morning, I wanted to head for home, but I decided to give the journey one more day, though it seems like an impossible plan to be able to make it to Eden and stop papa on my own. Maybe I'm crazy.

My fresh food is running out. After last night, I live in fear of being alone in the dark, and sunset is approaching. I don't know whom to trust.

Up ahead someone has made camp. A fire flickers. I can smell the smoke and cooking food. As usual, I'm hungry. I have money; maybe they'll sell me a meal. My coins are distributed, hiding among my sparse belongings, but I keep a few in a small purse in my pocket so I won't have to reveal where I've stashed the rest.

We approach the small camp. There's a large tethered grey mule, and a small figure crouching by the fire. A woman? No, it's a man. An old man. We draw closer and he stands and looks at us, then gestures for us to approach. A very, very old man. He doesn't look too threatening.

"Hello, good sir," I say in my best boy voice. "I don't wish to bother you, but would you please sell me a meal? I have coins."

The ancient's face examines me, then Midnight. He breaks into a smile. No teeth. A web of wrinkles. His skin is darker than mine. He's easily eight hundred years old.

"I've been waiting for you young...man. Go tie up that horse of yours."

I'm a little startled by this reply, but that baking fish smells delicious. Night bows and I climb off and tether him by his new mule friend. I carry my belongings over by the fire and drop them in a heap.

"How much for a fish?"

"One brass coin for two fish. One tonight, one in the morning."

"You don't mind if I sleep here?"

"No, and I won't even pick your pockets or steal your horse while you sleep."

I don't have any idea what to reply to that candid, but seemingly honest statement. Finally I say, "Thank you, I was a little worried."

"I know."

"You were waiting for me?"

He taps his head. "I have very good sight."

"Hmmm."

"Come sit down, my boy."

"I think I need to walk just a bit. I'm sore from riding."

"Off you go."

I walk around the horses and into the trees. I need a private minute.

The sun is disappearing as I return to the fire. The old man is spearing a fish and putting it on his plate. Travelers carry their own metal plate, cup, and eating utensils. I fetch mine from my pack, along with my small water skin.

I offer the old man an apple from my food bag. He accepts it despite his lack of teeth, and puts a large fish on my plate. It's filleted open. The skin is crispy, the inside tender. I am in heaven. We sit and eat. Growing up in the palace, I'm not used to being this hungry, and nothing has ever tasted this good -- salty and smoky and meaty.

"This is delicious, thank you."

"No problem. It's as easy to cook for two as one." He's cutting his apple into very thin slices, which are quickly disappearing down into his stomach.

I take the last few bites of fish then feel I should continue the conversation.

"My name's Egypt."

"I'm Mahujael."

"I have an ancestor named Mahujael. I think he was my great great grandfather."

Mahujael's eyes twinkle. "Good name. All Mahujaels are handsome and noble."

I laugh. "Yes, I can see that's true."

"Where are you headed?"

"West."

He examines me through the twilight and smoke. "Who's your father?"

This is a common, but tricky question. Because the Caananite tribe doesn't intermarry with other tribes, the families marry and intermarry with each other until all of us are related in some way or another, and everyone can figure out who everyone else is. I give him the name of my mother's father. "Geth."

All he says is, "Hmmm."

Then he offers, "Well, I'm tired. Us old people need a lot of sleep."

"Us young people too."

"Goodnight."

"See you in the morning."

Mahujael rolls up in his bedroll. I wash off my plate with water from my waterskin, then roll up in my own fur blankets. I can hear the river and crickets. And Mahujael snoring. I am not alone tonight. 'Thank you, God.'

I smile and fall asleep.

HAM: It's evening. The kingdom of Heni is prosperous. Its ocean ports foster a lot of trade. The mild weather fosters a lot of socializing and hedonistic living. If any group needs to hear Father's message, it's this one.

We arrived this morning in the main port and set up our stalls, though it's not market day. Even so, Father's caravan is famous enough to draw a crowd. He wants to move on as soon as possible, and travel lighter; so he's having us sell for coins only, instead of trading for more goods, as we usually do.

I've sold another stallion -- Cinnamon. A fine horse, broader and a little shorter than the others. Good for distance, and very well trained. He brings a good price. I have five left to sell. I pat Cinnamon goodbye and think about Midnight. Is he with Egyptus? I wish I were with her. I want to hold her and see her smile. I sigh. Cinnamon is led away. One more loss.

I look up to see Father watching me. He's been quiet and thoughtful since we left Nod. He seems worried. Maybe it's just the coming flood. After we left Egyptus' town, he sent his most trusted servant Kahleel on an errand. He didn't tell me why, but Kahleel hasn't returned yet.

The people are now gathered in their market square beside the sea to hear Father. I take the platform first and the waves are my drums as I strum the lute and sing to my Egyptus, so far away:

"I love to listen to your voice.
I close my eyes, it is so nice.
I love your shape, your face, your hair,
But by your voice I know you're there.

"I love to hear you in the hall.
When I come in, my name you call.
 I love to see you dance and walk,
But more, I love to hear you talk.

"It's true whenever we're apart,
I miss your sound with all my heart.
But yet no matter what life brings,
You say 'I love you' in my dreams."

The crowd cheers with loud applause. I smile and bow, but I just want Egyptus. My heart is no longer here, performing for them. It's with her.

EGYPTUS: The breakfast fish is just as good as the dinner fish. I'm still very sore, but I can tell that my body is adjusting to the change in routine.

Mahujael has put the fire out and has his mule packed up before I'm back from my morning "walk." I hurry over to him and offer him a coin. "Thank you for everything."

He looks at the coin doubtfully. "I don't need that, you gave me an apple."

"No, I insist."

"It was a mighty fine apple."

He starts to walk away, leading his mule, then turns and adds, "Hippo and I are also headed west. If you find me later we'll share another fish."

"Okay," I reply a little forlornly. "Go with God."

I load up Midnight and we head west down the trail. Night is a fast mover, and all day I expect to catch up with Mahujael. I see more washerwomen and pass other travelers. We stop very briefly for lunch and a leg stretch. But it's not until we're approaching the base of the mountain range at twilight that I see a flickering fire, and a large grey mule, and a tiny old man with a big, toothless grin.

I hop off Night, and with a big grin of my own say, "Hello, Hippo. Good evening, Mahujael. My that fish smells good."

Chapter Eight

EGYPTUS: In the morning, Mahujael and I enter Sharon on foot, crossing the high path over the gorge while leading our horses by the bridles. He says he doesn't want either of us falling over the edge if our animals bolt.

NEHOR: So far I see no signs of war. We have been crossing Sharon for a week. Some days we go farther than others, depending on where an inn is located. Mesael is taking advantage of the lack of men. There are plenty of pretty women in Sharon. At his request, once I'm king here I'll declare that we Caananites can marry with any tribe we please. These women are indeed pleasing, and apparently pleased with Mesael and his money.

Nabal and I are taking notes about possible invasion strategies and defenses. If we could manage to keep the men away, as they are now, this country would be an easy conquest.

EGYPTUS: We ride one day into Sharon, then spend the next day camped, as it is the Sabbath.

Mahujael begins to teach me to fish with his weighted net. It is round, about the length and width of three tall men -- or women, if you count me. Stones weight the edges. It is heavy and must be cast out flat and low over the water.

As it sinks, the fish are trapped underneath. After that you can spear them -- don't cut the net with your spear -- or wade out and fetch them with your hands -- watch out, they're fast and slippery. I finally find a use for my short sword. You only get one chance to throw the net, as the fish are spooked after that.

I practice throwing it in the field wherever we're camped. Mahujael catches all the fish the first week. I do learn to fillet them, light a fire, and cook the fish over coals. Even with me as chef, they're delicious.

I brew us mint tea in our metal cups. Mint is easy to find along the riverbank. We trade with the women of Sharon for spring produce: mostly garden greens, radishes, strawberries, and asparagus this time of year; and for unleavened bread, honey and cheese. I miss Adah's raised buns.

The women and children are very friendly. They're used to Caananites passing through as their land borders both Nod and Shum. We do hear that three Caananite men have traveled through a few days ahead of us. I am not anxious to catch up with and pass them yet. By following them I know where they are and what they're up to.

Mahujael is good company. He's full of stories about all the famous people who've lived during the last millenium. He has quite the memory.

HAM: Father seems to be in a hurry. The next market day finds us in Orlah, the capitol of Omner. This is a region where silver and other ores are mined. A lot of metal goods ranging from jewelry and swords, to building tools and cooking utensils are produced here, though they are vastly inferior to the metal products Shem produces at his forge. One of his magnificent swords can sell for as much as one of my horses.

Usually when we are here, Father orders a load of iron ore shipped to the ocean port in North Hanen. Then it's shipped up the Green River to the Ark's construction site, where Shem turns it into nails and hinges, along with finer things.

But today Father still just seems interested in selling, rather than buying or trading.

He has us sell all the mules, as we now have fewer goods to carry, and mules are slower than horses. I sell two more of my stallions – Sky and Flash. Sky has the best temperament and is the most easily trained. Flash is the fastest. A rich young man who aspires to be a horse breeder, like myself, buys them.

If he attends Father's lecture tonight, he'll find out that he doesn't have long to achieve his dream before the flood comes. Father is doing his best to invite people to repent and head to the Ark, but it seems like the more powerfully he gives the message, the less people want to listen to it.

I sing for Egyptus again that night. I must be getting morbidly depressed. My song is about death.

> "If I should die tonight,
> My love will still burn bright.
> In flesh I love you now,
> This flesh will die somehow.

> "But spirit I'll still be,
> My love inside of me.
> Alive forevermore,
> Eternal, true and sure.

> "And when you lay aside
> Your body and reside
> With me in Heaven's dawn,
> Our love bond will shine on."

The crowd loves it. I hate it. I want Egyptus now and in the flesh.

EGYPTUS: I catch my first fish after a week of practice on land and a few tries on the river. I don't know who's more proud -- Mahujael, or myself.

We eat my catch that night joined by Jom, a local boy headed toward the Sharon army with supplies for his father. Each day we are getting closer to the soldiers' huge encampment, which is on the other side of the Gold River in Havilah territory.

We've heard from the locals that the fighting recently ceased, at least temporarily. After two months of skirmishes, and the Sharon army advancing into Havilah, this is a huge relief to the families of Sharon, almost all of whom have someone with the fighting force.

To avoid the armies, Mahujael plans on detouring us south along the Sharon side of the Gold River, crossing west alongside the gold mines in Havilah, then heading back north to the Silver Pison River. He says he's going all the way west with me, at least to the Blue Hills, where he has business with the giants. I don't know which path papa and the uncles are taking.

Chapter Nine

NEHOR: We ride straight through the melee of tents and horses and men that comprises the Sharon army. The camp is huge, covering as far as I can see in all directions. It seems that at least a fourth of the entire population of Sharon is here: all the men of the country. This vast force needs to be reduced if we are to invade.

We are stopped multiple times by guards and soldiers along the way, questioning our presence. That's the disadvantage of having dark skin -- you don't blend in. Or maybe it's an advantage.

Mesael is our voice: "The noble King of Nod has arrived to offer his assistance to his ally the King of Sharon." We are allowed to pass.

The green banners of Havilah are everywhere. The tents are a miss-mash of sizes and colors, but they are in orderly rows and blocks according to the family, city, and region of the soldiers.

That makes it possible for those coming in with supplies to find their family members, and for news to be taken back and forth.

We keep heading west, as directed by the guards. With the frequent stops, and the vastness of the camp, it's late afternoon before we arrive at the royal encampment. We haven't brought an entourage or even a tent with us. That's a bit embarrassing.

We dismount and our presence is announced inside the King's imposing tent. We wait outside patiently as he prepares to greet us. Finally he emerges: a tall, thick man with reddish-brown eyes, hair and beard. Tall, thick guards surround him. All of them are wearing green tunics. The three of us bow deeply. He bows back.

"Greetings Nehor."

"Hello Aesel, how are you?" We shake hands.

"Oh, we're camped here in limbo while a treaty is negotiated. Come in the tent. Rest. We were about to eat."

Food sounds good. We enter and sit at a long makeshift table made of planks. I am seated at Aesel's side. We converse as dinner's served. It's pretty much the same thing we've been eating in the Inns along the way: fresh greens and berries of the season, venison stew with carrots wintered over in the now-softened spring earth, and wine.

Aesel tells us of the peace treaty that is close to being signed. This dispute is about the gold mines in the hills to the South. It seems that the Havilans have been mining for centuries, and dug so deep into the hills that they were burrowing on the

"Sharon" side of the Gold River, which divides the two countries. Sharon just wants its share, and it obviously has an army big enough to take it.

The negotiations are slow, as emissaries have to ride back and forth between the two encamped armies with their rulers' written offers. Aesel is expecting Harlan, King of Havilah, to send another reply in the morning. His troops will withdraw if Harlan will give him half of the gold produced from now on. He will even send workers to help in the mines.

We talk and drink until late, then are led to a tent for visiting dignitaries, where our bedrolls have already been laid out. "Well," I say to Mesael and Nabal, "it looks like we might be here a while."

HAM: I think Father has gone mad. He pushes us through the land of Enoch from early morning to late at night. He does stop to sell goods on market day in Trevillan, Enoch's main city. Kahleel, Father's chief servant, finally joins us again in the market at Trevillan. He and his horse look exhausted.

Father preaches in the city right after the market closes, instead of waiting until evening. Still, a significant number of people hear him. They seem either amused or bored by his message.

I don't play my lute. Just as well. All my songs are about missing Egyptus. Or worrying about Egyptus. Or longing for her.

We're packed and head west as soon as he finishes preaching. Since Father has only been selling goods, and not buying or trading for anything new, our horses' loads are becoming lighter, and his bag of gold heavier.

I leave another stallion behind in Trevillan -- Paint. He's brown with spots that look like white paint splashed all over. I need to think of more original names for my horses, but after seventy years of breeding them, I'm running out of ideas. Especially since almost all of Thor's offspring are male.

By nightfall a mountain range is in sight. Tomorrow or the next day we'll have to cross it into Shum. At Father's pace it will be tomorrow.

NEHOR: We've been here for days. The emissaries have been back and forth three times. Harlan offers peace for a one-time payment of gold. Aesel counters with forty percent of the mines' future production, plus the workers. Harlan offers to buy the land adjoining the mines so there is no question about whose kingdom it belongs to. Aesel considers attacking again. It just goes on and on.

Meanwhile, the soldiers are restless. They want to go home to plant their fields and continue their lives. Mesael, Nabal, and I are restless too. We want to move on and start our immortal lives. Mesael is especially going nuts without his required excess dosage of wine and women.

Finally at dinner I say to Aesel, "My friend, I came to help, and so far I've done nothing. Allow me to go with the emissary tomorrow and talk to Harlan. Maybe I can work out a deal in your favor, or at least find out what he wants."

Aesel runs a stout hand through his rust-colored hair and nods. "Well, he won't talk to me. And the peace process isn't progressing. If he won't negotiate with you, I'll have to attack again. I'd rather not, since it would mean losing more men. Will you go in the morning?"

"Of course, and I'll try to return quickly in the afternoon or evening to let you know what he says."

EGYPTUS: We have given the encamped armies a wide berth and slowly traveled south alongside the Gold river. It is a rough trail, steep in spots, and well-forested as we approach the hills. Finally we are at the base of the Gold Hills, named for the productive mines within them.

We cross over the river into Havilah. It seems quiet. All the miners have gone to fight. Rumor has it that King Harlan has drafted all the men in the kingdom into the army. We certainly don't want to risk being inscripted despite our dark skin. We will travel carefully, avoiding any settlement or signs of civilization.

HAM: We do cross the West Enoch mountain range the next day, descending in the late evening and camping on the foothills. In the morning we awaken in Shum, or rather, Father wakes me up just at first light. "Ham, come look," he says.

We leave the tent and walk to the edge of camp. I look out over the dry plain. At first I see nothing unusual through the lightening gloom. Then Father points and I see them. A chill goes through me. These are foreign. I've never even heard of them before. In the distance, from the north, two giant white bears are ambling slowly through the flat plain -- easily visible. Huge deer-like creatures with thick, branched horns follow them. Trailing behind are smaller ground creatures rustling through the sparse new-grown grass. The animals are headed for the Ark. Tears well up in my eyes. We're running out of time.

I look at Father. "What are we going to do?"

"They are travelling slowly. We've got to move quickly and prepare the Ark," he looks at me, "and you've got two more horses to sell."

"Who cares about the horses? We can go south from here to Nod, get Egyptus, then head over the pass to Cainan. We'll be home in two weeks, maybe less."

Father sighs and shakes his head. "Let's go wake up the camp."

The camp is already stirring and we're quickly fed. Father has a long conversation with Kahleel while we pack. Kahleel is a believer and wants to go with us on the Ark, but only if he can get his family to come. If they won't, he's decided to stay and drown with them. Father hands him a leather bag that obviously contains much of our gold.

He walks back to me. "Call Spirit and Star."

I whistle for my two remaining stallions and they trot up to me. Thor comes too.

Father asks, "May I ride Star?"

"Of course."

I'm a little confused but watch as he bridles him then boosts himself up on the beautiful white horse. His own riding horse, Ben, is loaded up as a packhorse. Kahleel has been organizing the other servants and horses into two groups.

Jarom and two other servants on horseback join Father, along with Ben and two more packhorses carrying goods to sell, plus our tent.

I mount Thor and settle my bedroll and pack in front of me, as usual.

Father waves to Kahleel. "Good luck," he calls, "God protect and guide you."

"You too," Kahleel calls with a wave, "go with God." He and eight servants turn south toward Nod with the rest of the packhorses. Father and the remaining three servants and horses head west. Spirit, Thor, and I catch up with Father.

"What's going on?"

"Kahleel is taking the gold back to the Ark. He'll warn the family that the animals are on their way and have Shem and Japheth hire as many men as they can to finish whatever isn't done on the ship and load up before the rains come."

"What about us?" I am very confused.

"We're going to Shermaal to sell Spirit and Star." Shermaal is on the western edge of Shum, close to the base of the Titan Mountains -- The Uncrossable Ones.

"Why?"

"I'll tell you after you sell the horses."

"Well okay then." I turn and ride at the back of the pack. Frustrating. I really need to get Egyptus from Nod. It will take days to get to Shermaal.

We soon cross paths with the animals headed to the Ark. Up close the bears are terrifying. Huge. White. Long black claws. They pay no attention to us at all. God will protect them on their journey. May He protect us too, and Egyptus.

I begin to pray silently. It calms me as we cross the wide, wide plain of Shum.

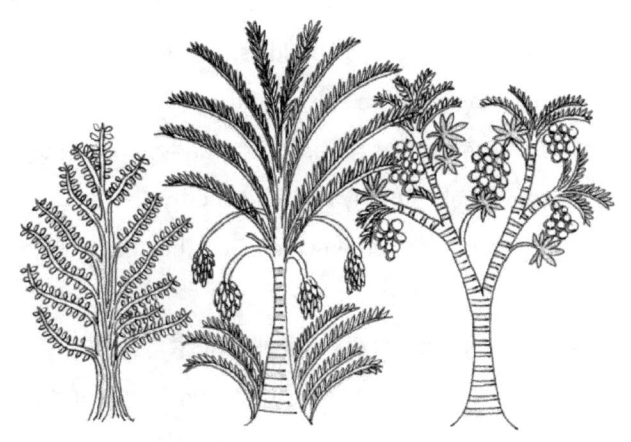

Chapter Ten

NEHOR: The emissary and I set out early the next morning. By mid-day we're led through the gold-bannered army camp of Havilah, announced, and ushered into Harlan's tent.

Harlan and I have met before, but it's been a long time. He is young for a king -- : only in his second century. He reminds me a little of Ham: muscular, tall, and slender, but with longer blond hair than Ham, plus a short beard. A gold tabard belted at the waist covers his tan clothes. We bow to each other. The emissary hands Harlan the scroll with Aesel's latest peace offer. Harlan reads it then tosses it into the corner with a "Humph."

He crosses his arms and looks at me. "What are you doing here, Nehor?"

Given that three centuries ago my grandfather Lamech took over the country of Shem, driving out or killing all the inhabitants, including Harlan's family who had fled and settled in Havilah, we had never been good buddies.

"I'm here to negotiate an end to the war."

"Great. The ruthless warrior's grandson has come to negotiate peace on behalf of my invading enemy."

"Well, justice was served when God then cursed the land of Shem. It's barely been fertile since."

"But still, the tribe of Caanan inhabits it."

"Look, we can rake up ancient history, or we can sit down and you can hear what I have to say. In private please."

Harlan looks at me steadily. I stare back. Finally he says to his guards, "Search him for weapons, then leave us." I am thoroughly searched. My sword is removed, and the knife in my boot. They retire from the tent and we sit at a small table.

"Do you have a map?" I ask. Harlan fetches one from a nearby box and unrolls it on the table.

"Look," he says, "I'm sick of that stupid army being on my land, wanting my gold."

"Good," I say, and smile. "We're going to get rid of them."

"How? They outnumber us two to one."

"I've been with them a few days. I've got it figured out." I point to the map. "This is where they're camped. Tonight you're going to send a fourth of your army south, into the forest at the base of the Gold Hills, far enough away that Aesel's army won't know they're there, and his army will think they can retreat that way."

"Retreat?"

"Yes, because tomorrow night another quarter of your army will stay here in this camp, west of Aesel's army. But the other half will retreat a short way farther west up the Pison river, cross it, then come back down and hide in the forest on the other side of the river north of their encampment. Half of that contingent will wade across the river downstream and circle around to the east side of the camp, arriving just before first light.

"At that time I will sneak into Aesel's tent and stab him through the heart. Better yet, we'll stay up all night celebrating the peace offer he sent you today, which you will have 'agreed to' and signed. Then I'll be right there to stab him.

"With the first ray of the sun, your troops attack from the north and east. Sharon will have no leader because the King will be dead. Everything will be confusion.

"The Sharon soldiers won't be able to retreat past your soldiers back east into Sharon. When they go west, they'll meet your soldiers attacking from your camp. So look," I point on the map, "they'll go south, where your men will attack them from the forest there.

"They'll be surrounded by your men on all sides, and your soldiers will slaughter every last one of them. Problem solved. No one will ever attack you again."

Harlan doesn't move, just stares at the map. Finally he looks up. "You are the very Devil himself. Why would you do this?"

"This fall I want to invade Sharon and rule it for myself. This way I'll pretty much be able to walk right in."

"Then I'll have a devil for a neighbor."

"I'll make a covenant with you that I'll never invade Havilah as long as you or one of your descendants reigns. Besides, with Aesel on the throne you already have a devil for a neighbor."

He thinks about it, not realizing that someday I'll kill him and his descendants, *then* I'll invade Havilah.

"Agreed." We shake hands.

Harlan says, "Stay here until tomorrow. You can return mid-day with the signed treaty. The whole camp will start celebrating and drinking into the night. They'll all be incapacitated when we attack, as well as having the confusion of a dead king."

"Good job. Now you're in the spirit of things."

Harlan smiles. We discuss details of the carnage ahead. The unenlightened emissary is sent back to Aesel to inform him that my negotiations are progressing, but that I need more time.

Harlan calls in his Generals. They all discuss the plan and decide which troops will go with each General in the different directions.

The oldest and most suspicious of them looks at me. "How do we know we can trust him?"

"We don't," Harlan replies. "But he has much to gain if this works, so I think he'll do his part. All he has to do is tell a big lie and kill a king to gain a kingdom."

The General shrugs then says to me, "Okay. But if they're forewarned when we get there, we'll attack anyway, and I'll personally hunt you down and kill you. You'll be easy to find with your dark skin."

I smile. "Agreed. But you can be sure I'll do my part. I like this plot a lot."

EGYPTUS: I roll over and wake up. It's pitch black except for the stars peeking through the trees up above.

Something is out there rustling. It sounds like men and horses, still far away, but approaching. What to do? We need to leave. I go touch Mahujael and wake him up.

"Someone's coming," I whisper.

He whispers back, "Quick, get the gear. Leave no trace but the cold fire."

We stuff our packs and grab the animals' lead ropes. I throw Midnight's bridle over my shoulder. Mahujael is loading the bundled net and his pack onto Hippo. I secure my pack and our sleeping rolls on Midnight, then follow Mahujael as he heads up the hill behind our camp. We each lead our steed by the tether rope. It's steep, but do-able.

Soon we are up above the forest floor and the muffled commotion below. What is going on? Mahujael climbs and climbs. I follow through the darkness. Finally daybreak arrives and we stop. We're almost to the top of the hill and can see the sunrise over the valley below.

I take the horse and mule and secure them to a nearby tree then join Mahujael, who is staying out of sight, but trying to figure out what's going on. I see the sun flash off something below. The old man turns to me.

"I think that's soldiers and horses down there."

"Really? From which army?"

"I don't know, but I think we're stuck here until they leave."

I sigh, "Great."

I'm hungry and still need sleep. I retreat and unload the steeds, piling all of Mahujael's things together. I search through my pack and find the dried fruit and bread I've carried from the palace. I haven't needed them until now, as we've caught fresh fish, bought produce, and foraged for greens.

I nibble on the dried food and drink from my waterskin, then take some over to Mahujael, who's still watching the valley. No news. I go back and roll up in my bedroll and finish my night's sleep.

NEHOR: So far so good. I returned late this afternoon with the signed peace treaty. Everyone rejoiced. A very few men packed up and headed for home, but almost all stayed to celebrate. Lots of laughter. Lots of wine. Even some music and dancing.

We've been imbibing with the King and his Generals. Mesael would like more wine but is cautious, like Nabal and I, to look much more intoxicated than he really is. It's getting toward morning. Time for death and destruction.

The guards are lolling by the tent entrance, not quite passed out. Aesel is singing off-key hugging his wine skin, and his army friends aren't much better. Two are completely asleep.

We draw our daggers. Nabal and Mesael stab two Generals just before my knife enters Aesel's heart. I twist and pull it out. One guard comes at me from the tent opening, obviously confused. I slit his throat. No alarm sounded. My brothers have finished off the sleeping army leaders. There's a little bonus for Harlan: no king, and no leaders for the army either.

I kill the second dozing guard then wipe the dagger on his shirt. I am so good I don't even have blood on my hands. My brothers have cleaned their blades too.

Nabal makes a slit with his knife up the back of the tent then pokes his head through. "It's clear," he tells us. "Look drunk. Quiet, but drunk." We step through the slit then drunkenly weave to our borrowed tent. We've already packed, so we grab our bags and bedrolls and drunkenly weave to the horses stationed in the nearby corral.

I find Ahab and jump on. Mesael is already on Firelight. Nabal has decided to go for an upgrade and is on Aesel's big red horse Granger -- a mighty beast indeed. Probably one Ham sold him. Totally recognizable, but who cares? Aesel won't be coming after us.

We open the paddock and let ourselves out. We need to go west until we're out of the encampment, then turn south toward the Gold Hills, then when we're far enough that we won't be trapped between the two warring armies, head west again toward the Misty Blue Hills where the giants live. Right now I just want to get out of here before the battle starts. We've got about an hour before sunrise, then the fun will begin.

EGYPTUS: "Wake up, wake up," Mahujael is shaking me. "Something is happening below."

I follow him to the lookout spot. It's full morning. I've slept in. It felt really good. After yesterday's nap, I wasn't sure I'd sleep all night, but I did.

Sure enough, there's a commotion below. Men shouting, things clanging. It sounds like an army loading up for war. Far across the valley there's movement. A swarm is headed our way.

"Oh my goodness," Mahujael laments. "This is an enormous battle."

"Do we need to load up and leave?"

"No, I think this is the safest place we could be."

We watch. My heart is thumping fast. Sure enough, when the swarm has come closer we hear a battle cry from below, and a cloud of mounted and unmounted soldiers emerges from the trees below us, running full speed toward the advancing swarm. The swarm sees them and stops, but they have no where to go. They're surrounded on all sides by a sea of gold.

Then the battle begins in earnest. An entire army fighting for its life. We can make out tiny figures of men and horses falling. Dying. It's awful.

I turn around and lie down, looking up at the sky. "Tell me when it's over." I try to hear nothing, and think of the words to Ham's songs, my mother's lullabies, the story of Enoch. Anything to distract me.

It seems hours later when Mahujael says, "I think it's over." I dare to turn around and look. The plain is littered with death. Thousands and thousands dead. Fathers and sons not going home.

It's quiet now. The winners, those left alive, aren't even cheering. They appear to be picking through the dead for spoils or walking northwest toward Havilah's army camp. I guess Havilah "won."

Mahujael says, "Let's stay here today and leave in the morning. Things should be settled down by then. We'll want to leave before the miners return."

"Okay."

I'm heartbroken. I spend the rest of the day meditating and praying. So many dead. So many more yet to die in the coming flood.

Chapter Eleven

HAM: We arrive at Shermaal the night before market day and make camp. The unending heat every day while crossing Shum has sapped our energy. Even the horses are exhausted. I think that if he could have, Father would have had us sleeping on our horses and never stopping at all. The five of us are in the same stuffy tent and practically pass out from exhaustion.

In the morning we head for the market. Father instructs us to sell everything we can except for what we need for the ride home. We'll keep only our riding horses, including Ben: and the tent, food, bedrolls, and personal items.

I go to work and sell the two packhorses and Spirit, the beautiful grey stallion. Surprisingly, it's a girl who buys him: a beautiful young girl with dark skin, like Egyptus. The three servants sell everything else.

Father continues his uncustomary ways and stands up on a box in the middle of the square, preaching repentance right during the market. People shake their heads or ignore him.

"Have you seen the strange animals passing through here two by two? They are going to my Ark. Please follow them. Come, so you won't drown in the coming flood. Please, at least repent of your sins, so when you do die in the storm you'll be acceptable to God. Do good to others. Be kind. Follow His commandments."

It's no use, but at least he tried. That's a prophet's job after all.

As market ends, Father comes over to us. We are packed and ready to go. "What's that?" he says, pointing at Star.

"It's a horse."

"What's it doing here? Why isn't it sold?"

"I guess he's just being an unsold horse."

"Then sell him to me. How much is he?"

"I was asking twenty gold coins, but for you, ten."

"Okay." Father pulls out his moneybag and counts out ten gold coins. This amuses me, but I go along with him and take the money.

"Okay, now we can talk," he says, then turns to Jarom. "Take Ham's pack and load it with food. Find him a coat and his sword, lute, and bedroll. And have Thor ready to go." Jarom bows and walks away.

"Come with me." Father goes over to sit on a bench in the middle of the dusty square. I sit by him. He begins: "Egyptus came to me in the morning just after you left the village of Enoch. Her father and uncles had discovered a map that would lead them to the Garden of Eden and the Tree of Life. They soon left to try to find the Tree and eat its fruit, thus becoming immortal. She decided to follow them to try to prevent or reverse their immortality.

"I found an old friend to keep an eye on the situation. Surely you remember Mahujael? Kahleel returned with him to Nod.

"Egyptus is dressed as a boy and has a map I drew her. She'll follow the Silver Pison River to Eden. Mahujael followed her, intending to join her and travel with her as a protector and guide.

"Kahleel saw him on his way, watching over Egyptus from a distance on her first night alone, then made sure that she was travelling with Mahujael before he left them. Then he met us in Trevillan to give me this report. Now, you need to make it across the Blue Hills past the giants into Eden, find Egyptus, prevent any fathers or uncles from becoming immortal, and make it back to the Ark before the flood."

The old man has completely lost it.

"What?"

"Egyptus, Eden, Ark. You can do this."

I stare at Father in disbelief.

"Why didn't you tell me this before?"

"Egyptus and I had an agreement that I could tell you only when you sold your last horse. Now it's sold."

"Yes it is." I say, bemused. "But aren't there guards at the Garden of Eden? Surely they'd stop the intruders."

"They could unknowingly hurt Egyptus too," Father warns.

My heart lurches. The rabbits. I need to be there.

"So, goodbye?" I ask. My Father has always seemed strong to me, but now he seems a bit frail as I put my arm around him. I remember that he's turning six hundred years old soon. He should be able to spend his birthday at home, if he hurries.

He says, "You must go out on your own now, like those stallions you breed, to find your path and form your own family. Bring Egyptus to the Ark. I'll see you there."

"Do you think there's enough time to do all this?"

"There will be with God's help."

I'm overwhelmed but manage to say, "I love you, Father. Tell Mother 'hello,' and give her a hug from me."

"And I love you too, Ham. Go with God." He stands and walks over to the servants. Taking my baggage and Thor's reins from Jarom, he walks back to me. "Here you go. Have a good trip."

"Thanks. Go with God, and Happy Birthday." I'm still in shock, but I stand and we give each other one last hug. Then I secure my belt and sword around my waist and leap onto Thor. I settle the bundles in front of me and ride toward the west. As I leave the square I turn one last time to see Father and the servants waving goodbye. I wave back and they're out of sight.

NEHOR: My brothers and I ride west following the Pison River. We must cross the Havilah valley to the Misty Blue Hills. From there the river winds through the hills until it comes out in the land of Eden. But we know the hills well because the giants are our allies, and they are always good for some fun and entertainment. Mesael is especially looking forward to a visit to the giants' main village -- Midgard.

We find ourselves sleeping in the open because the Inns are full of Havilah's soldiers returning to their homes. I am looking forward to Midgards' accommodations as much as Mesael is to their alcohol and other amusements.

Chapter Twelve

HAM: All I have to do is cross straight west through a short stretch at the northern border of the Misty Blue Hills along the base of the Titan Mountains, and I'll be safe in Eden Valley. The giants won't follow me there. If I'm lucky, I'll make it across in one day.

I tell myself this as I cross the rest of Shum after leaving Father. At twilight Thor and I make camp at the foot of the Blue Hills. Their grey rock base makes them look blue from a distance, and they're mostly foliaged with huge trees. Farther south from here the ground is thermally active and sends out waves of mist from hot pools of water and steam vents; just another danger in this wilderness of lions and giants. I'm definitely not going farther south.

I spend an uneasy night.

Thor and I start out early the next morning. We approach the hills. Thor doesn't like them any more than I do and is skittish as we approach and begin to climb.

"What's the matter, Thor?" I pat his neck. Probably he's just sensing my nerves. It seems quiet here. We pass through the towering forest. Maybe this far north the land is uninhabited. I don't see signs of chimney or campfire smoke. No sound of drums. We haven't crossed any clear trails, but we're not stopping for anything.

Thor and I continue over and around three hills, then four. It's midday now. Thor suddenly stops, his sides heaving as he smells the air. I look carefully around through the trees, trying to sense whatever has disturbed him when suddenly I'm on the ground, twisted in a rope weighted on both ends by stones that has been thrown and wound around me.

I struggle to sit up, but before I can stand and leap on Thor to gallop away, two giants are standing over me. "It's Big Grey," one of them says.

I can't understand how people can be so tall. And muscular. You can see their bulging muscles from their square jaws down to their square toes.

One of them pulls me to my feet and the top of my head comes to his navel. The other isn't quite as tall. I come a handspan above his navel. They wear leather and fur and have fuzzy beards and hair-covered bodies. I suppose leather doesn't wash well and giants don't either, because they smell terrible. Like giants. No wonder Thor was spooked.

They're both staring at me.

"Must be Noah's kid," the big one says.

"The King will want him," the bigger one replies.

"Yup, let's go." With that they remove my sword, secure my ropes, and throw me stomach-down over Thor's back. This is not comfortable. I hope we don't have far to go.

But we do. We travel south all day. Then they lay me on the ground to sleep tied up all night. I do talk them into letting me stand up to do my business in the morning. No privacy though.

Then it's tied up on Thor's back again and all day we cross south. Sometimes I can smell the sulfur odor of thermal pots bubbling from the earth. They rival the stink of the giants. Occasionally I hear distant drums.

Where are we going? Oh yeah, to the King. Why? Probably to kill me. After all, the giants have tried to kill us before. Why? Probably some old beef they had with an ancestor of mine. I don't know. All I know is this is seriously delaying my trip to Eden, and I'm hungry and really sore from riding Thor in a way he wasn't supposed to be ridden. My feet are hanging on one side, my head hanging over the other. I think I'm going to be sick. Only I haven't eaten for almost two days, so there's nothing in my stomach to throw up. Great.

It's evening when we reach what seems to be their main encampment. From my upside-down vantage point I see that there are tents everywhere. I guess they live in tents. Maybe that way it doesn't hurt when they hit their heads on the ceiling.

We stop. More giants come over to look at us. I'm pulled off Thor and can't find my feet so land in a heap by my horse. Now I'm just mad. Oh yeah, and surrounded by big, stinky giants. The smell is nauseating, but I'm so very hungry that I could eat despite the smell.

These people don't talk much, do they? They're staring at me, and at Thor. Even Thor looks uncomfortable.

"You found Big Grey.

"And Noah's son."

"My name is Ham."

"He talks."

"Yes, you should have heard him this morning. He wouldn't shut up until we let him relieve himself." Wow. Bigger just said more than three words in a row.

"Let's take him to Vanir."

"He'll be happy."

Great. I have an audience with a large, stinky, fuzzy King.

Big takes my ropes, Bigger leads Thor. My feet are untied and we are walking along the north edge of the tent village. Oh, we're entering an actual wooden building. Hope the ceilings are high enough. Yep. High ceilings. Thor is brought in too. Plenty of room for my very tall horse.

We're led to the main table at one end of the massive structure. Apparently feasting is happening, but that stops with our arrival. The King looks up. I can tell he's the king because Big and Bigger and everyone else bows to him. I choose not to bow.

"We found Big Grey," Big says. Vanir suddenly looks very happy. He stands and walks over and strokes Thor's mane.

"Big Grey!" he booms and hugs Thor's neck. "You're finally back!"

Back? I'm more and more confused.

"And here's the thief who stole him," Bigger says

Vanir turns to me, "Death to the thief!"

"Wait!" I interject. "I don't understand. Thor is your horse?"

"Of course he's mine. He's the only horse in the world big enough for me to ride."

That makes sense, actually.

"I didn't steal him. I found him by Eden Mountain. He must have wandered away from the Blue Hills. The grass is very lush in Eden. We used to live there, remember? He wouldn't even let me ride him for a year. You're lucky I found him. Look, I've taught him a lot of tricks and commands. I'll teach them to you and you'll have an even better horse back again. Is that why you've been trying to kill us? Because I had your horse? I am so sorry." I finally stop talking.

The King looks at me carefully. I can tell he's still thinking of killing me. Maybe charm will work. I smile and say. "Thor, bow to the King. He's missed you." Thor does a deep bow. "Now shake hands and say you're sorry for running away and you'll never do it again." Thor lifts one foreleg and extends it to Vanir. The King bursts out laughing, then everyone else in the room laughs too. I give a sigh of relief and start breathing again.

Vanir cuffs me on the shoulder. Ouch! "Okay, boy, you are forgiven too. You can start teaching me all these commands in the morning."

Now I bow. "Of course, your highness."

The feasting resumes and I'm untied and get a seat between Smelly and Smellier, who apparently are noble folk, since they are at the King's table. Everything served seems to be made of meat. Large chunks of meat. Smaller bits of meat. And is downed with alcohol brewed from who-knows-what. After a sip I ask for water. It comes with dust floating on the top, but oh well; at least I'm not hungry or thirsty any more. Or dead.

114

The mood is jovial and I'm halfway through my third chunk of meat when the doors open again. More visitors. More greetings. I stop mid-bite. Why, that's Egyptus' father! And her uncles! This could be good or bad.

I decide to make it good. They've greeted Vanir and I rise and go over to bow to them.

"Nehor! Mesael! Nabal! It's so good to see you!" I turn to Nehor, "How is your family?" Nehor stares at me, completely shocked. I've sure been stared at a lot today. I try again, "Tell me, was Egyptus well when you left her?"

Nehor gathers himself. "Yes, I left her in charge of the palace." He turns to Vanir, "Do you know that this is Noah's son? I thought you hated Noah's family."

Vanir shrugs. "Apparently we had a misunderstanding. We're good now."

Nehor turns and looks at me. I grin. He shakes his head. "Well, do you know that he's a musician? You should have him play for you."

"Really," Vanir says. "It seems he has many talents. We never have music here. Just drums. That would add to the party." He turns to me. "Will you play for us, boy?"

"Sure," I say. I think I've had enough meat wads and slime water for now. "I'll get my lute."

My plate and cup are cleared off the table and space is made for the three new arrivals as I walk over to Thor. Luckily my pack, sword, and bedroll are still secured to his harness. I'm surprised that the giants haven't taken my sword, as Shem made it, so the quality is unmatched, but maybe it's too small for them to be interested in.

Thor nudges me and I pat his neck, 'I'll get us out of this. I don't know how, but I will. Sorry, boy.'

I untie my equipment and lead him over to a giant who appears to be a servant. It's hard to tell servant from master, what with their fancy, furry clothes and all. I hand him the reigns. "Will someone please take this big grey horse out where he can eat some grass, or something? The servant nods. Vanir has been watching this exchange, but seems to relax when he sees Thor led away by the servant.

I drop the rest of my things in a corner and return to the table with my lute. "Now how about a song about a horse?" I ask, and proceed to sing them the filly song. I can tell they're more used to stories than music, but they like the song.

Mesael has already had a lot to drink in the five minutes he's been sitting there. He raises his cup. "How about a drinking song? Sing about the joys of alcohol!"

"No," calls Smelly, "I want one about Dragons!"

"Dragons?" I muse. "You mean the mythical, large, flying, fire-breathing creatures whom stories say live in the Titan Mountains?"

"Yes, those Dragons."

Hmmm. Large and small humans are looking at me, waiting for me to decide who wins. I strum a bit, then begin:

"Joel the farmer, so drunk he wobbled,
Into the woods one night he hobbled.
He had his dog and a skin of wine.
Then he sat down and began to dine.
(On wine!)

"When along came a dragon so large and grand,
The ground shook as he walked on land.
The dog gave a woof, the man tried to hide.
It was too late, the dragon them spied.
(Then sighed.)

"Dragon licked his chops, he liked the taste,
Of men and dogs in his great big waist.
Though the man shrieked and the dog was hairy,
He crunched them up with teeth long and scary.
(Be wary!)

"He ate them up right in his belly,
Let out a burp, fiery and smelly.
The dragon exploded 'cuz he'd forgot,
That fire and alcohol explode when hot!
(A lot!)"

I've satisfied everyone. They cheer and toast my song. I get lots of requests and end up singing songs about Big Grey Thor the Magnificent Horse, Spring, War, The Sun and Moon, Lions (the Blue Hills have lots of lions, maybe that's why only large, stinky giants live here), and of course, Meat.

Then I wander over to the corner and put my lute away in its case in my pack. The table has drifted into conversation. Nehor is updating the giants about the war in neighboring Havilah.

I take out my bedroll, spread it out, and lie down. There doesn't seem to be anything in the conversation which affects my mission to Eden and Egyptus so I close my eyes, give God thanks for my continued mortal life, and go to sleep.

Chapter Thirteen

HAM: I'm awoken by something nuzzling my ear. It had better be Thor. I roll over and look up. It is. Apparently horses sleep inside the wooden tent. I look around. It really is massive. Giant sleeping bodies are everywhere. Oh, there's Nehor and the uncles, also asleep, and their horses. It's mid-morning. They were probably up late carousing.

I've slept at least twelve hours. I needed to. Between Father pushing us across Shum, then my restless night before the Blue Hills, then being tied up and hardly sleeping the night before last, I was exhausted.

I'm hungry, despite the odor of this place. I stand and Thor accompanies me over to greet Ahab, Firelight, and Granger. What's Granger doing here? He's Aesel's horse.

Maybe he sold him. I give them each a good rub behind their ears and pat their necks. They remember me and I get nuzzled. Thor greets them too. They are all his sons.

I head to the huge doors. Pulling one open takes a lot of force; they are so heavy. I walk through and Thor follows me. There's a guard right outside. He blocks us with his spear. Looking down at tiny me, he asks, "Where are you going?"

"I'm hungry. Is there food around here?"

"You can eat at that cooking fire over there, but the horses need to stay over in the paddock."

I look behind me. All four horses have followed me out. I lead them to the small corral by the wooden tent. Since the giants don't keep horses, or any livestock, this must be for visitors. They start eating the long grass as soon as they're inside.

I shut the gate behind them and head to the cooking fire. Once there, a woman shyly hands me a bowl of what looks like stew. A giant's portion. Yum. I look up and thank her. She has golden skin, green eyes, and medium-dark brown fuzzy hair in a thick braid down her back. She's slender but muscular and is wearing a loose leather dress secured at the waist with a beaded belt. She's magnificent, and she doesn't smell as bad as the rest of the giants I've met.

I like it out here. The air is fresh. There's sunshine, and three giant-sized tables surrounding the fire. I climb up on a bench and put my bowl on the table. I feel like a little kid on the high bench, and sit swinging my legs as I spoon fuel into my starving body. Looking around at the village, there are a few trees, but mostly it sits in a large clearing. About a hundred extra-large tents are here, spread out in semi-orderly rows. Surprisingly, a large, well-tended, fenced garden plot surrounds each one. It seems that the peas and onions in my stew are locally grown.

Women are about, tending the gardens or cooking over outside fires. Children my size are helping them or playing together in the paths. They give me furtive glances. Two young boys drop the firewood they've gathered and go over to stand on the paddock rails to see the horses. A male giant arrives at the cooking fire with a large deer slung over his shoulders. He soon has it hanging from a nearby tree limb and is gutting and skinning it. I don't care to watch, though that is probably my dinner.

I hear drums start up. Giants don't read and write, but all the sounds of the Adamic language have a drum pattern for them and they communicate that way. The sound echoes a long way through the hills. Probably the return of Thor is being announced. Who knows?

I've finished eating. I go wash my bowl in the nearby stream and return it to the gorgeous cook. "Thank you, that was delicious."

"You're welcome," she softly replies. She's too shy to look at me, but takes the bowl.

I head over to the paddock and stand on the fence with the boys. They are both slightly taller than I am. Golden skin. Fuzzy brown hair. One has brown eyes, the other hazel. To me the giants all look very similar, but their eyes are all different colors.

"Hello," I say, "do you like the horses?

"Oh yes," says Brown Eyes, "I want one someday."

"Me too," says Hazel.

"I'm Ham, son of Noah, and I raised all these horses, except for the big grey one; he's their father."

"That's the king's horse, isn't it?"

"Yes, but he's been with me for a while." I whistle and Thor comes over.

"Want to pet him?" The boys pet his neck. They don't seem afraid of him, as most traditional-sized human children are.

"Want to ride him?"

"Oh yes!" they both chime.

I walk around to the gate and we go inside the paddock. They are sturdy boys and weigh more than I do, so instead of boosting them up, I show them how to climb on the paddock rails, then onto Thor's back from there. Brown eyes goes first. He tells me he's named Sig. Once he's on, I walk in circles along the fence, and Thor follows. Then it's

Hazel's turn. He's named Ymir. This is good fun. They both take a turn on the smaller Firelight. While we're occupied with this, the giants and Caananite royalty are waking up and eating their breakfast at the cooking fire. I'm showing the boys how to command the horses to do tricks.

A few giants come over to watch. Vanir arrives. "I see you started without me," he says.

"Come on in," I gesture. He enters the paddock, and Thor and I spend most of the afternoon teaching the king tricks.

EGYPTUS: I am really scared of giants. And lions. I don't know which are worse, and the wilderness of the Misty Blue Hills is full of both. Mahujael assures me that the lions are far worse than the giants. That's such a comfort.

He reminds me that since the time of our second father Cain, who often lived with them, the giants have always let members of the tribe of Caanan pass through their land.

When the King of Nod, my great grandfather Lamech, took over the land of Shum hundreds of years ago, the two tribes then shared a common border in the northeast, further cementing the friendship. No other tribe passes through.

We have traveled half a day into the Blue Hills, roughly following the Pison River. There are no clear paths through this forest wilderness. The thick green canopy of huge trees blocks the sun overhead. It smells musty and wet. Hot steam wafts from the earth here and there. Scalding thermal pools of water bubbling from deep in the earth add to the danger of the hills. The sounds around us are strange. I hear the frequent skitter of small animals, foreign bird calls overhead, and drums…strange. Mahujael has been here many times. I ride Night closely behind him and Hippo.

Suddenly a giant steps from behind a tree, blocking our way. My heart stops. I'm going to die of fright. I'm frozen and can't even scream; I just stare at the huge creature approaching Mahujael. Then they are speaking to each other but I can't hear them. The blood is pounding too loudly in my ears -- apparently my heart is beating again.

The giant looks at me, then steps back into the trees. Hippo is moving forward and Midnight follows him. I am breathing too quickly, but I *am* breathing. Terror sweat is drying on my body, making me cold.

I tell myself, 'It's okay, Egyptus, see? Mahujael was right. The giants aren't going to kill us.' I feel lightheaded with relief. Giddy almost.

Soon we join the river again and stop to eat. We sit on rocks and watch the water drift by.

I state, "I've never seen a giant before. What did he say?"

"That one's name is Askr. He says that we'll have to stay the night at Idum village up ahead."

"Why? Can't we just sleep out here by the river?"

"No. The lions would attack the horses and us. I guess they find horses tasty. The giants don't keep livestock for that reason. They just forage in the woods, hunting along with the lions."

"Why don't they just kill them?"

"Sometimes they do, if they are annoying. Mostly I think they find them useful, as they keep us mere humans from invading their territory."

Hmmm. "The giants are descended from Adam too, right?"

"What makes you think that?"

"They speak Adamic."

"True. I think you just solved an old puzzle. I've always wondered where they came from."

We mount up and Mehujael turns to me. "I told Askr that you are my grandson."

"Okay, lead on grandpa."

Mahujael laughs. We continue on.

As we are skirting yet another hill we hear a terrifying growl. All four of us freeze, then Midnight scuttles beneath me. "Whoa, boy."

We are all looking for the source of the sound. We've found it. Three lionesses appear: two over the top of the ridge and one to our right.

Before we can do anything, an arrow whizzes by our heads and a huge, golden cat rolls down the ridge and lands dead at our feet. The other two cats disappear instantly. Askr appears from the trees behind us and goes over to nudge the dead feline with his foot.

"Excuse me," he says, "do you mind if I take this home to Embla?" I look into his deep blue eyes, which are on a level with mine, and shake my head.

Mahujael bursts into laughter. "No, my friend, and perhaps we'd be safer if we followed you home."

Chapter Fourteen

EGYPTUS: We arrive at Idum late in the afternoon. The giants live in tents -- really big tents made of leather; some are simple, and some are shaped quite fancifully. There are twenty or thirty here, with a large wooden building in the center. It is a very pretty spot surrounded by the forest. The gardens are neatly kept around the tent houses: a profusion of bright, fragrant roses and other flowers growing along with the vegetables. If it weren't full of scary giants, I'd like it.

"Why is there a wooden building?" I ask Mahujael as we approach.

"It's their community center. The king stays there when he comes. Everyone retreats to it from lions or other dangers. It's used for feasting on marriage days or holy days -- all purpose."

Everyone is openly staring at us as we enter the hamlet. They all look like Askr, who leads us.

Mahujael pauses and greets the first giant who comes over, "Hello, I'm Mahujael of the tribe of Caanan. This is my grandson Hujah."

"Greetings, Mahujael and Hujah. I am Ragnar, village Chief. Welcome to Idum."

He walks alongside Mahujael, who is still shorter than he is, even riding on Hippo. They are chatting as we trail behind Askr, heading to his home.

I try to take in this strange world as we follow him. Everything is huge. At the far edge of the hamlet, we stop in front of a tent with a domed top. There are triangular yellow flags wafting from its four corners. A woman is cooking at the fire in front of the home. Askr smiles at her and says, "Look what I brought you."

"A dead lion, and little people. They look hungry."

"Well, at least the cat isn't hungry any more." He lowers the lion off his shoulders and onto the ground.

Ragnar introduces us to Embla as we dismount.

Mahujael smiles at Embla and bows. "I am honored to meet you, gracious lady. Your husband said we could find hospitality in your lovely home."

She smiles and sighs, "We don't have visitors often enough for Askr. He loves to bring strangers home. Says they're interesting."

"Our King has visitors too," Ragnar tells us. "The King of Nod has come again, with his brothers. They passed by here yesterday on the river trail to Midgard, but didn't stop."

Embla responds, "Maybe they'll stop on their way back to Nod." She turns to us. "Are you two from Nod?"

I'm frozen and can't respond. Father is near. What if he discovers me?

Mahujael finds his voice. "We are indeed from Nod, madam. But alas, from a village on the eastern bank, so we do not personally know our dear king."

"Well, maybe you'll get to meet him. Are you going to Midgard?"

"Hujah and I have yet to choose our path for tomorrow."

Ragnar inserts, "You should go. The king has finally recovered his big grey horse from Noah's son and is having a celebration feast tomorrow. The drums have invited all that want to attend. Several of us are heading up in the morning, almost all of the men, anyway. There will be contests of strength and archery, and lots of food and drink. Askr, do you want to come with our party? We need you in the archery contest." He indicates the dead lioness, with the arrow piercing her heart.

Askr looks at Embla.

"Off you go," she says.

I have a terrible feeling in the pit of my stomach, but venture to ask, "Noah's son? There's a Noah who comes to preach in our village. What does the king's horse have to do with Noah?"

"Oh, Noah stole the animal years ago. It's big, grey, and shiny. A head higher than any other horse. We've all been on the lookout for it ever since. We almost got it back once; we nearly killed Noah and his whole family, but they escaped. Now it's back, along with Noah's son. Bet the king will kill him for taking it. Can't let a thief live."

I feel faint so sit on a nearby rock and put my head between my knees. Mahjael comes over and puts his arm around my shoulders. "Are you okay, son?"

I nod, my head still down. My voice comes out muffled, "Yes just too much sun today, I think."

'Don't cry,' I tell myself. 'Don't cry, don't cry.' I breathe deeply.

Mahujael stands up. "I believe my grandson is tired from the journey, which has been long. Perhaps there is a place he could lay down? Then I could tell you all about the battle we witnessed a few days ago between Sharon and Havilah. Ragnar, I think you will find it to be a splendid account, one you'll find worth repeating."

Mahujael fetches my bedroll and pack from Midnight, then helps me up. Embla leads us into the tent. I'm in shock and don't notice anything around me. Mahujael spreads out my bedroll in the back corner and I lie down. Soon I hear their voices outside by the fire and I turn over and cry and cry.

It's dark when I wake up. Mahujael is shaking my shoulder. "Egypt, wake up," he whispers. "Come and eat, then I'll tell you my plan."

'Plan?' I'm groggy. My head feels stuffed up. Everything comes back to me. Oh, yeah, it's stuffed up from crying. All of those tears watering my brain.

"Okay." I say, and listlessly stand up and follow Mahujael through the tent. Outside the air is dark and crisp and smells like cooking fire.

"He's awake," Embla says. "Come sit down here by me, dear child." I guess I do look small and child-like to her.

I climb up by her on the high bench. Mehujael joins Askr on the bench across the table. There's a cold plate of food waiting in front of me: fish and greens. They've all eaten long ago, when the food was still hot, and have obviously been enjoying each other's company. Mahujael can be very entertaining.

"Eat up, son," Mahujael says.

I pick up the fish and find that I'm hungry after all. "Did you catch this Askr? It's very good."

"Yes, I did. In the river close to where I found you two."

"Embla, you must have cooked this. It's even better than grandpa's fish, and his is the best I've ever tasted."

"Why, thank you, Hujah."

Now that I've made an effort to appear social, I continue eating and worrying about Ham. The two men are discussing the coming joys of the king's feast.

Mehujael finally turns to me, "Hujah, I am going to Midgard with the men tomorrow morning, but Embla has offered to guide you to the Eden border. From there you can follow the Pison River to Eden Valley to retrieve your father's flock where the winter shepherd has them grazing."

He turns to Askr. "I don't know what my son was thinking, putting them to pasture so far away. By the time Hujah gets them to market down south in Ethiopia they'll be skin and bones."

I think of a fast reply and play along. "Grandpapa, you know no one has ever grazed sheep in Eden Valley. With all the wars going on, Eden is the safest place, and the grass is lush and untouched. The spring lambs will make us a lot of money. In a few years we'll have hundreds of sheep there. We'll be wealthy. Papa is a great innovator."

I turn and continue, "Embla, when I come through here again, I'll bring you a couple of lambs. They make delicious stew."

Embla replies, "I'm afraid for you. The valley and plain are cursed."

"For giants, but not for Caananites."

"Well, if you hear God's voice rumbling from that evil Eden Mountain, you get out of there, sheep or no sheep."

"I will."

Askr adds, "Embla, you shouldn't tell our friends where you've led him. I don't mind you showing him to the border; it's a mighty crazy thing, but they're paying you well, and we can use the gold. I just don't want everyone thinking we have anything to do with that cursed place."

"No need for anyone to know. All you men will be gone anyway, and I'll be back before nightfall."

I question, "Speaking of nightfall, where are the horses?" Midnight is nowhere to be seen.

Askr replies, "Ragnar took them to the wooden tent to spend the night; lions, you know. He sure enjoyed your war story, Mahujael."

"Yes I've never seen anything like it -- thousands dead." He turns to me. "Hujah, would you like to walk down with me to check on the steeds before bed?"

"Yes, grandpapa."

We rise. I thank Askr and Embla again for the excellent meal. We go through the fence gate and head down the uneven path in the dark, going slowly as there's little light from the heavens to guide us.

When we're out of earshot I whisper, "So I'm going to Eden?"

"Yes, and I'm going to Midgard with Askr. I'll send Ham and if possible, Thor, on to you."

"What? What do you know about Ham and Thor?"

"I know that Ham is your beloved, and that Noah wants you both on the Ark. I know the flood is coming soon, and that you might not make it there in time without Thor's strength and speed. Egyptus, I know you're a girl."

Oh my goodness. I feel faint again, and spying the outline of another available rock, I go sit down, my head between my knees. I must have had too many shocks in the last few days.

Mahujael sits by me and starts patting my back. After a few deep breaths, I sit up.

"How do you know all this?"

"Noah told me."

"So Noah sent you, a perfect stranger, to watch out for me?"

"I'm not a perfect stranger. I've kept an eye on you ever since you were born. I keep an eye on all my descendents possible, and there are many, many of you. I'm your great great great grandfather."

"Oh my goodness." I start crying. Again. I seem to have crying days, and this is one of them.

Mahujael pats my back some more. When the crying doesn't stop, he starts rubbing it. "Come, come now child. It's going to be okay." I eventually run out of tears.

"You're still alive? How old are you?"

"I'm not sure anymore. Over a thousand, I guess. I couldn't figure out why God was leaving me on the earth for so long, still spry and healthy. Then when Noah found me and explained what was going on, I realized that God had one last mission for me.

"Egyptus, I'm here to help you get on that ship. If you don't, you'll drown with all the rest of the Caananites, the giants, and all the other tribes. The world would be a very uninteresting place without our people. They will add strength and goodness and beauty to it. They will be leaders in art and music and show others how to be happy."

"How do you know all this?"

"Well, they'll be descended from you, possibly the most strong, beautiful, and good person I know."

"And the art and music?"

"Oh, that's from Ham, despite the fact that our tribe has invented every musical instrument, including his lute."

I sniff and give a watery giggle. "This is a big responsibility."

"Take it one step at a time, my dear. Now tomorrow you're going to follow Embla to the Eden border. Once there, you'll give her the gold coins we'll put together for her. On Eden's plain you'll head north until you find the Silver River and follow it west. It will take about two days to get to Eden Mountain. It sounds like your father and uncles will stay for the feast tomorrow night, so they won't be leaving for two or three more days. Hopefully you can find a way to stop their immortality then head for the Ark."

"I will do my best grandpa, thank you." I give him a hug, my first grandpa hug ever. It feels wonderful.

He steps back and looks at me. "Egyptus, after you leave tomorrow, I won't see you again until we meet in the world of the spirits, where we'll stay until the resurrection. After that, we'll be immortal together, and we'll have lots and lots of time for more adventures, but I've sure enjoyed this one with you here on earth."

There is a long pause as I collect my emotions, then tearfully I reply, "Me too grandpa. It will make a good story to tell the other immortals. I wish you could come on the Ark with us."

"Well, you can tell me all about it when I see you again."

I nod, trying not to think of this separation. I need to stop crying. "Okay."

"And when you see Rose on the Ark, will you tell her 'Hello' and that I'm so proud of her."

"Rose?"

"Yes, Roseta, Seth's wife. I was her tutor when she was growing up in Assyria."

"Really? You just keep surprising me tonight."

"Well, Rose can tell you all about it."

We link arms as we stand and slowly walk the rest of the way to the wooden tent. Poking our heads in the door, we see that Hippo and Midnight are fine. We re-latch the heavy door closed. My tears have finally dried up.

We link arms again as we idly walk back to Askr and Embla's home, grandpa telling me family stories the whole way. I find out that I've had some "interesting" ancestors.

Chapter Fifteen

NEHOR: I'm bored and want to be on my way to immortality, but Vanir insists that we stay for the feast tomorrow, and Mesael isn't about to miss the celebration. I'm beginning to suspect that Mesael's realized that alcohol won't affect his immortal body like it does now, and he's having one last binge. I look down the table at him with his cup of hooch, sitting on a giantess's lap, and I shake my head. Amusing, but pitiful.

"Sing us a song!" Mesael calls to Ham, who's sitting cross-legged with Sig, the King's son, on his bedroll in the corner. They are playing some kind of game, and marking points with white and black rocks.

"Yes!" Vanir calls. "Music please, Ham."

Ham looks up upon hearing his name and appears at the table with his lute a few moments later.

"What would you like to hear tonight?"

"Something for this beautiful woman," calls Mesael, "this beautiful rose of a woman."

Ham perks up a little. It seems like his is heart just hasn't been here today. He seems to feel like I do: wanting to move on.

"A rose, huh? I know a love song about a rose, will that do?"

"Sing! Sing!" Mesael demands.

"Okay." Ham has a trace of a smile as he plucks the strings then begins an old-fashioned melody. This familiar folk song is hundreds of years old.

"There's a rose in my garden,
There's a rose in my garden,
I planted it there,
See the flowers it bears.
There's a rose in my garden.

"The red rose in my garden,
The red rose in my garden,
Is for passion so bright,
That is shared in the night.
The red rose in my garden."

There's a lot of whooping after that verse. Ham strums an interlude until it settles down.

"The white rose in my garden,
The white rose in my garden,
Is for love true and fair,
Like a lad would declare.
The white rose in my garden.

"The pink rose in my garden,
The pink rose in my garden,
Is the love I have for you,
A combination of the two.
The pink rose in my garden."

"Here! Here! Very nice," calls Mesael, amid the scattered applause.

"Let's let Sig choose the next song," says Ham. All eyes turn to Sig, who has been listening in the game corner. He thinks for a minute.

"How about one about travelling? Us giants never get to go anywhere but the Misty Blue Hills, and sometimes to Mount Herman."

"Okay," Ham nods and begins a light, floaty melody. Sig stands up and creeps closer. Ham smiles and sings to Sig:

"If I could sprout some wings and fly,
I'd go see all the world:
The ocean, and the surf and sky,
The seashells tightly curled.

"I'd see the fields with fruit and grain,
The towns with markets big.
The sheep and cows out on the plain,
And horses with their rigs.

"I'd fly 'ore forests, snowy drifts,
And jungle river drains.
The deserts with their colored cliffs;
That's where it never rains.

"I'd see Mount Herman from the top,
But I'd be missing you.
So I'd fly back, and here I'd drop,
To tell you of the view."

There's much cheering. Ham bows to Sig and pats him on the back. Sig is very pleased; he obviously has a huge case of hero worship for Ham. They go back to the corner. Ham is showing the boy how to hold the lute and play simple chords. The rest of us are drinking and laughing, but I'm bored and want to leave.

EGYPTUS: Mehujael wakes me up before it is light. We pack my bag. Inside I have my change of clothes, the urn lid, some money and jewelry to trade for food and lodging on the way back to the Ark, and a bit of dried food.

I dress and buckle on the belt with its short sword. Mehujael gives me his moneybag with long drawstrings, which I hang around my neck under my tunic.

Pulling on Ham's coat, I stick my hand in the pocket and pull out the red scarf with the gold embroidered edge that Noah gave me to cry on. It's clean. I should have used it to catch my flood of tears yesterday.

I hold out the scarf. "Mahujael, will you take this to Ham? He knows it's mine."

"Good idea," he says, and puts it in his tunic pocket. I pick up my bedroll. Mehujael has given me all of the food and all the money. He says he'll make do.

We head out into the cool pre-dawn air and walk to the wooden tent. Mehujael goes inside and brings out Night, who is wearing his harness strap and reign.

I attach the bedroll to the steed's back, and the pack to mine, then take his leads and we start walking back to the tent to meet Embla.

This is goodbye. I'm keeping my eyes dry, but my stomach strangely feels like it's crying. I can do this. I break the silence and murmur, "Thank you, Mehujael. I wish I'd known you longer."

"You will," he replies.

"I know. When you see my mother, will you tell her that I love and miss her, and that I'm still a believer?"

"Of course, I'll tell her how wonderful you are, and all about you and Ham and our recent adventure."

"I'm sure you will. Thank you. Tell her that I love you too. I couldn't have made it this far without you." We hug tightly.

"I love you too. Go with God, my dear child."

He steps away. Askr and Embla are coming out of the tent door. They embrace. Embla has a short sword like mine strapped on, and a large bow and arrows, as well as a spear as tall as she is. She looks fearsome.

Askr says to Embla, "See you tomorrow."

"Yes, hopefully not too late," she replies.

I give Mehujael one last hug and wave, then Embla and I head west down the path, in the opposite direction from the wooden tent in the center of town, and are quickly in the woods. It's barely getting light, just enough to avoid the tree stumps and follow Embla's lead.

She turns and says, "Why don't you get on the horse's back? We'll be able to go faster."

"Okay." Night bows and I climb on. She's right. She and Night can walk faster.

Deeper in the woods she becomes chatty, telling me about her family, and that she'd like to have children. "None of

143

my babies have lived," she says. "It's hard to make a baby giant. They often turn out with extra limbs or deformed in some way. We're happy to get a baby with just extra fingers or toes. Something about being this large doesn't reproduce well. Everyone has trouble."

"Is that why there aren't many giants?"

"I suppose so. But once one is born healthy, they usually grow up strong and with few problems. We're confined to these hills though. Other tribes kill us if we leave. You're a good listener for a young boy."

"I just find your tribe interesting. Do you think we'll meet any lions?"

"They sleep early in the mornings. We're safe for now."

I ask about life as a giant, their customs and celebrations, courting and marriage traditions. From her reply it sounds like it's all similar to the other tribes.

I tell her about Mehujael teaching me to fish, and about Noah's preaching. "I'm sorry he is considered your tribe's enemy. You would have loved his message."

"He would have been killed here anyway. I mean, he's not a Caananite is he?"

"No, but I think prophets should be an exception. They belong to all the world."

"It would be lovely if all the tribes could get along. Then we giants could travel. I'd like to see the ocean."

"Me too. Until now I've never left the borders of Nod."

Embla pulls out bundles of spicy meat wrapped in lettuce leaves and hands me one. We eat while we're moving, then stop briefly for water at a stream.

The sun has passed its zenith when the light changes; the trees are farther apart. We come to the top of a hill, and a flat grassy plain spreads before us all the way to the horizon. It looks like an infinite green lake, as the gentle breeze blows the early summer grass in waves.

Embla looks over and smiles at me. "We're here." She points northwest. "That's the direction to go. By mid-afternoon you'll meet the Pison River. You know to follow it upstream. You'll see the trees growing along its banks before you see the river, and you'll be able to see Mount Herman to the north when you get to it."

"This is so wonderful." I've finally made it.

We go down the final side of the final hill. I feel like a bird landing on earth when we hit flat ground. Embla won't come all the way down because of the curse. I slide off Midnight and climb back up the short distance to her.

"Thank you, Embla. I can't believe that I'm really here. It's been such a peaceful trip. No wars. No lions."

"Just a giant, or in this case, a giantess."

"Yep, just a giantess. A great and kind one."

I lift my money purse from around my neck and take out the ten gold coins we'd promised her. I hand them to her and she smiles. It really is a fortune for a day's work, but completely worth it.

I say, "Thank you so much. You'll be safe on the way back to Idum?"

"Yes, child. I have my weapons and I know how to use them."

"Okay then. Go with God."

She turns and starts up the hill. I go down the short distance to Night, who already seems fond of Eden's lush grass. He lets me climb on and we're on our way. I pray fervently for Ham, Mehujael, and Thor with Midnight's every step.

Chapter Sixteen

NEHOR: The party has finally begun. A couple hundred visitors have come from across the hills to celebrate. In the afternoon everyone sits down around the paddock and Vanir and Ham show off Thor and his many talents.

Thor looks like a pony with Vanir on his back, but Thor can carry him, though Vanir's much heavier than Ham and Egyptus together; I know they've ridden him jointly before.

I contemplate Ham. He's too innocent and good. I will have no use for him once I'm the immortal ruler, except maybe as a court musician. After all, he is a clever and talented singer. We'll need some entertainment in my throne room. He's decorative too. And he could train my horses. Hmmm. Maybe he's more useful than I thought.

Right now the entertainment is an archery tournament. A giant from the village of Idum wins the gold coin.

Next come feats of strength. Spear throwing for distance, then accuracy. Arm wrestling. Leg wrestling. Log chopping. More gold coins. These contests go on until it's nearly dark.

All the tables from the village have been moved inside the central wooden building. Everyone crowds in and finds a seat, enjoying the food and drink. We'll be able to leave in the morning. I can't wait.

HAM: I'm packed and ready to go, except for my lute, which I need for this feast. My things are hiding outside in the woods, though I'll leave without them if I must. Tonight is my chance. All of the giants who are usually out in the woods hunting and guarding are in here.

I wish they'd get drunk, but liquor doesn't seem to affect them much. They must be too big and have too much muscle; it burns off too fast. I'll have to choose my moment carefully. Thor can outrun them. Maybe they'll get sleepy.

I eat my meat dinner with some humble villagers at a table on the far side of the room from the King. One of the villagers leans over to me.

"Hello, I saw you with Big Grey."

"I'm Ham, son of Noah."

"I'm Ragner, Village Chief of Idum."

"Glad to meet such an important person. Being a chief must be a lot of responsibility."

"Yes, I have to keep everyone up on the news, make decisions about safety: like if the weather is too bad to go hunting. I was just telling the tiny old Caananite that a storm is coming and he needs to get out of the Blue Hills by tonight."

"Where was he going?"

"He came north with us but then headed east to Havilah. He'll be able to get there before the storm."

"It was lucky that he had your wisdom to guide him."

Just then the King calls for Thor to be brought in the room. My handsome horse is fetched and led up to the King's table. He has a gold-trimmed red scarf tied jauntily onto his harness strap. Vanir gives a speech about how strong and fast Thor is, and how his capture has pleased him.

He leaves out the part about how smart and loyal he is. And how he ran away from this lion-infested wilderness eighty years ago. And how devoted he is to me. He probably would have already run away again if I weren't here. Thor is looking as inpatient and disgusted as I feel. I resist the urge to whistle for him. Then we'd see whose horse he really is.

Vanir calls me up to sing a celebration song. I pick up my lute and make my way through the tables to stand by Thor. All I want is my horse, my girl, and a nice, smooth ride to the Ark. I bow to the King, then begin one of the songs I'd sung my first night here:

"Is Big Grey Thor, the magnificent horse,
The very best steed in the world? Of course!

"Dragon for mother, father a giant,
He's large and brave and strong and defiant.
In danger and storms he continues reliant.
When we need a hero, he's always compliant.

"Thor's like a storm on Mount Herman's tall height.
His hooves sound like thunder, rolling at night.
His speed is as lightning, showing his might.
He'll win any race or contest or fight.

"And now here he is just gracing our feast.
Admired by all from the great to the least.
Only a king can ride such a grand beast.
All others who try will soon be deceased."

There's a roar of laughter from the crowd. I applaud Vanir, who stands to take a bow.

Then Thor is led out and I follow him to the paddock. The wind is starting to pick up. That's right, Ragnar says a storm is coming. There are a few giants outside talking; it's not safe to leave yet.

The three other royal horses are in the paddock with Thor. Surely in a while Thor wouldn't be missed.

I go in the paddock with him and untie the familiar red scarf from his harness. I smell it. This is Egyptus'. I recognize my favorite person's scent. The little Caananite man Ragnar told me about has to be Mahujael. He and Egyptus must be here somewhere.

I tuck the red cloth in my pocket and swing the lute by its strap onto my back. Leaving the small corral, I start walking around the giant-sized wooden tent. Sure enough, when I get to the back I hear my name whispered: "Ham...Ham..."

I go into the brush, and there he is: the tiny old man. He looks extra small to my eyes after being with the giants for four days.

"Mahujael?"

"Hello Ham."

"Where is Egyptus?"

"She's on the Eden Plain by now, crossing to the Valley and Eden Mountain. She's fine. We've got to get you and Thor out of here."

"I know Vanir thinks Thor belongs to him, but I don't think I can make it to the Ark in time without him."

"Obviously Thor is yours now. Anyway, we have to do what we must to save you and my granddaughter."

"Egyptus is your granddaughter?"

"Three greats. Are there still four horses in the paddock?"

"Yes."

"I slipped in earlier to tie the scarf on Thor. The giants who saw me just thought I was Egyptus' father or one of her uncles. To them we all look alike -- short and dark.

"I have a large grey mule. Not as large as Thor, but he'll do. I can wait until no one is paying attention then trade him into the paddock for Thor. That way there will still be four animals there if anyone looks. If I get caught trading them, I can say that I decided not to go to Havilah, or just take the blame for stealing. You won't be suspected, and can try an escape later. If I'm successful, you can take off on Thor."

"What about you?"

"Ham, I'm very old. My life is over. This is my last task. My future isn't on the Ark, so either I'll die in these hills, or in the coming flood, and I think I'd rather die here. I want you to promise me that you won't try to save me. I want you to go to Egyptus. Promise me, Ham. This isn't a decision I want you to make later, if I need to sacrifice myself for you or Thor. Promise me now. She's my only hope of my line continuing on. You must save my granddaughter. Promise."

I hesitate. He's so sincere. It would be like leaving a drowning kitten, but if I were he, I would ask the same thing.

"Okay. It will be hard, but I will leave you if I must. We'll always remember you, and your sacrifice, if it comes to that." Mahujael extends his hand. We shake on our deal.

"Thank you, Ham." A wind gust blows harder. Mahujael says, "I think God has a hand in this wind. Have you noticed the giants don't keep dogs?"

"I was told they keep no livestock because it would draw lions in to attack, but you're right, no dogs."

"They don't need them. They already have super-acute hearing and sense of smell for hunting. This wind will make it more difficult to track and find you."

"Come with me on Thor. I'd feel safer."

"I feel like that's a good idea. We'll meet you down the path that leads west in an hour or so. Whistle for Thor and we'll come to you. Go back now. Be visible. Sing. Whatever. I'll try to trade the animals."

"Okay. Let me get my pack, sword, and bedroll. You can take them for me. Then I won't have to try to get them on my way to meet you." I fetch my things from behind a nearby bush and Mehujael takes them and puts my pack on his back.

I turn to Mehujael and we solemnly shake hands. "I'm praying this works."

"Me too."

EGYPTUS: The wind is blowing hard. The sliver of a moon and its bespangled sky have slipped behind clouds now. The only shelter Midnight and I can find is in the trees near the Silver Pison River. I secure him to a thick trunk. He mustn't leave me in the storm.

Fetching my bedroll, I wrap up, covering my head and face. I sit leaning on the tree growing next to the one Night's tethered to, with my back to the wind. Night has his head down and his back to the wind also, so I spend the night with a view of his rump, and continue praying for Ham, Mahujael, myself, and our horses.

HAM: I sing. I'm visible. I'm charming. All while yawning occasionally. Finally I go to sit down near the door, and look sleepy. After a few minutes I turn my head and glance through. There are still four animals in the paddock, but now none of them is Thor.

I follow a giant out the door when he leaves to relieve himself in the nearby bushes. I head for a bush too, then go deeper into the woods and head west. Once I've gone a sufficient distance I quietly whistle. Thor comes, and I'm up on him behind Mahujael. We take off. The plan worked perfectly.

NEHOR: It's really late. Half of the giants are already asleep, either with their heads on the tables or lying on the benches or floor. Mesael passed out long ago in an alcoholic stupor. He doesn't look well at all.

154

The wind has stopped howling, but rain has begun pounding on the roof, which leaks in places. Vanir calls for Thor and the other horses to be brought inside out of the weather.

HAM: We ride through the miserable night until we are at least halfway to Eden Plain. We've decided that without sun or stars to guide us, we must follow the Pison River, or be lost or fall into a thermal pot. I give Thor his head, trusting him to find footing on the slippery path along the bank. We continue steadily. Mahujael says the lions won't hunt in the downpour. I was so worried about lions, but haven't seen even one during my stay here.

Finally the drums begin, though they echo faintly through the pounding rain. I can't read them, but I know what they're saying: "Find Big Grey, Find Ham." We have a good head start. All we can do is continue.

Toward morning the rain becomes lighter. The path and trees are first blacks and greys, then take on color as dawn arrives. The drums continue: "Find Big Grey, Find Ham."

Mehujael and I leave the river path now that we can tell which direction is east from the cloud-shrouded dawn. We climb a hill and then at the top of the ridge we see there is only one smaller bank of hills to go over and we'll be safe on Eden plain. I point silently and Mahujael nods. No use attracting giants' ears.

Down the hill we go. Crossing a small creek, we head up the next, last, smaller rise. Almost there. But suddenly there is a giant blocking the way in front of us. I kick Thor's sides and he takes off. We whiz past that giant then two more. Over the top of the hill we go, and down the other side. We've outrun them all!

Except for the bunch near the bottom with bows drawn. "Whoa," Mahujael says, and Thor stops, the three of us breathing hard. Mahujael snaps the reins and we canter up into the clump of giants, almost passing through them, but the leader reaches out and grabs the bridle.

"Hello, I am Ham, son of Noah," Mahujael says.

"Get off Big Grey," The leader growls, his attention on Mahujael. We dismount, and as soon as my feet hit the ground I run for flat land. In five leaps I'm at the bottom of the hill, running on the cursed Eden soil. I whistle for Thor and hear a yelp and a thump. I grab Thor's mane and swing on as he whizzes by me, and we are flying so swiftly, I don't think Thor's hooves are even touching the ground.

I hear the giants' yells of anger, Mehujael's whoops of triumph, and a few arrows landing harmlessly in the grass far behind us.

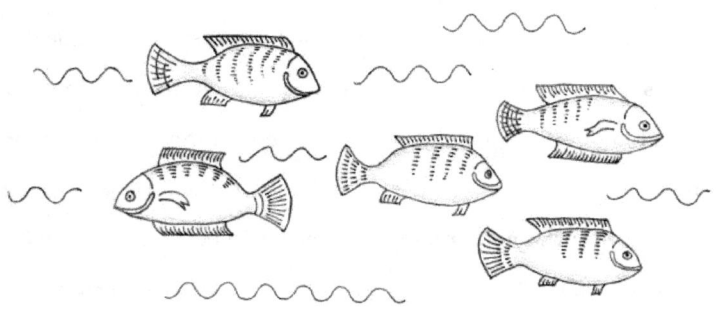

Chapter Seventeen

EGYPTUS: I follow Noah's map to the farmhouse, which is glowing gold in the light of the sunset. Talk about overgrown. I guess I shouldn't have expected anything less after seventy years of being unoccupied.

The house is stone, with a solid slate roof and thick wooden shutters and door. There are some very determined climbing roses clinging here and there to the walls, happily blooming in pink.

I contemplate Ham's birthplace and childhood home. It's quite charming, even in this wild state. I could be happy living here with him. Too bad it's going to be washed away soon.

I sigh and dismount, taking my baggage off Night's back. He wanders a few feet away and begins to munch the grass and weeds. At least one of us has something to eat.

I lift the latch and push the heavy door open. It's very dark inside so I go to a window and push open the squeaky shutters. Midnight briefly lifts his head to look at me then goes back to grazing. I sigh again. I can't decide if I'm more hungry or more tired.

I'm in the main room of the house. There's a stone oven to cook in, and a heavy wooden table and five chairs near the window. Everything's dusty but I sink into a chair and set my pack on the table. Opening it I take out my few belongings, hunting for anything to eat.

Hallelujah. There are a few raisins in the pocket of my spare pants. I eat them one at a time, making them last. Then I spread out my bedroll on the dirty floor and lay down. I miss Mahujael.

Gold light turns pink then silver as it falls through the window. I close my eyes. "Goodnight Midnight," I murmur out loud. I'm asleep before I hear his answering whinny.

HAM: We're getting close to Eden Mountain but it's too dark to go on. Mahujael's net was attached to Thor, along with my own belongings. This afternoon we stopped and I used his net to catch some fish: five with one throw. They're practically tame in this uninhabited country. I gutted and cooked them all.

Now I eat my fill of leftovers and roll up in my blankets. The stars are brighter here than anywhere in the world. It smells like fresh grass, and from the munching it sounds like Thor's trying to eat a whole valley's worth in one night. Egyptus must be near. Surely I'll see her tomorrow.

It feels good to be clean. This morning I bathed and washed all my clothes in the river, but my sheepskin sleeping roll still smells like stinky giants. Ugh. That is enough to inspire bad dreams. I decide to dream about Egyptus instead. Thank you Mehujael. Thank you God.

EGYPTUS: I awaken to silvery light and a roof over my head. Rolling over I stare at the flagstone floor, at the heavy wooden beams overhead, the rock walls. This is a very sturdy house.

My stomach growls. I need food so badly that I'm surprised that it has enough energy to growl. Well, I'm not going to find nourishment lying here. Rising, I roll up my bed and tie it closed. I go to the front door and whistle for Midnight.

He comes trotting around the house. His mouth is red. So are his teeth. "Night, what have you been eating?

He trots back around the house and I follow. Three ancient cherry trees tower in the field behind the house. "Oh thank you God." I'm about to have a terrible stomachache from an overdose of cherries. I couldn't be happier.

I munch contentedly beside Midnight. The fruit is sweet and juicy. I feel its energy start to sing in my veins and laugh out loud. Night looks at me and snorts. Finally I am full. The sun comes up and a warm ray touches my skin. I'm going to live another day.

Running around the house, I enter and stuff my belongings back in my pack and fasten on my belt and sword. I pull the window shutters closed, grab the bedroll and pack, then exit and make sure the heavy door latches behind me. I give the door a pat. "Thank you house. Thanks for the roof last night. Thanks for sheltering baby Ham. You are a sacred place to me."

I head back to the cherry trees and fill the top of my pack with the shiny red fruit. Night is back to consuming grass. It looks like I'll eat cherries until I'm sick of them.

"Let's go find the Garden, if it exists, Midnight." He hears his name and trots over.

I'm beginning to doubt that the Garden can be found. It seems like a dream after this long journey. My father and uncles are no more than two days behind. That's a nightmare waiting to happen. I need to find the entrance to the Garden today, or at the latest tomorrow, or else I'll end up spying on them, watching to see if they can find it. Then what do I do? I have no clue.

"Well, Night, at least we can do what the urn lid says. Let's go to the east of the mountain and bow." Midnight hears the word *bow,* so he bows for me and I hop on his back.

Eden Mountain can't be missed. It juts straight up from the ground. Its dark stone walls support nothing but the most obstinate foliage. As it looms closer, I become more and more nervous. It just looks like a mountain, but what if it's not? What if I die because I step on forbidden, holy ground? How close do I go before bowing?

A thin waterfall leaves a silver trail down the middle of the east face. Very scenic. Clumps of trees shelter a clear pond at its foot. Pink, lavender, and red flowers decorate the surrounding banks. As we approach, the falling water grows louder.

Midnight must be thirsty because he's headed straight for the pond. Seems like a good idea. We pass between the trees and stop on the sandy beach. I hop off and bow deeply to the mountain. Midnight wades into the water and begins to drink. "Hey, where's your bow?" He ignores me.

I kneel and scoop up water with my hand and drink. It's delicious. Kind of warm. Perfect for bathing. Hmmm. The lid said: "Wash before entering."

I look down at myself. I'm covered with dust. My clothes are sweat-stained and grimy. I smell like me, only multiplied by sixty. I'm disgusting. I take off my boots, then look around and shrug. As far as I know, the nearest humans are a day away.

The rest of my clothes come off, down to my breast binding. I struggle with it but am too impatient, so toss the clothes in the shallow edge of the pond. Then I grab my pack and pull my spare outfit and Ham's coat from underneath the cherries and throw them in also. I find and place a stone on each piece of clothing so they won't drift away while they soak.

Wading in deeper, I find the water is heavenly. Clean, pure, refreshing, but warm enough to be pleasant. The constant din of the waterfall masks all other sound. The human world feels so far away. It seems I've found my own Eden. I dive and swim, then float on my back. The sun is higher and warmer now. I close my eyes against its brightness.

HAM: Such a beautiful day. Such a beautiful valley. Childhood memories come flooding back. Here's where Shem, Japheth and I played and grew. Across the fields lies our farmhouse. Our sheep grazed here close to the pond and river.

I found Thor in the dell over there by the mountain. He was the only animal we'd ever seen living here in Eden. Wild animals must sense the place is cursed, like the humans believe. It took me a year to gain his trust, train, and ride him. I pat Thor's neck. We are moving quickly toward Eden Mountain. Hopefully we're the first to arrive.

Thor's ears twitch. I can make out an animal in the pond at the base of the waterfall. It's a horse. A dark horse. It's Midnight! I slow Thor down. If there's an owner with the horse it has to be Egyptus -- I hope.

Stealthily, Thor and I approach the pond from behind the trees. Someone is swimming. They roll over and a flick of a backside appears out of the water then disappears in a dive. It's definitely Egyptus.

162

Relief and joy flood me. Without thinking, I ride Thor into the pond and dismount into hip deep water. Egyptus surfaces near me and the look on her face as she sees me becomes one of total shock, then she lights up with pleasure, then she starts crying. Wading toward each other, we're in each other's arms rocking and laughing. She has a few teary sniffs left in her.

I bend down and kiss her lips. Cool and wet, but delicious. My hands slide down her slippery back. She pulls away, her eyes round.

"Oh my goodness, I'm practically naked! Turn around!" I laugh, doing my best not to look at her goodness. "Turn around!" I comply and hear her sloshing toward shore. Then there's more sloshing.

"How long have you been here?" I query, examining the waterfall in front of me.

"I just got to the pond. I slept in your farmhouse last night."

"Can I turn around now?"

"No! I'm having trouble getting this binding off."

"Want some help?"

"Ha ha. Very funny."

I smile to myself. There's still more sloshing. Dressed or undressed, she's got to be the loveliest thing on earth.

"Okay, you can turn around." I do. She's on shore, dressed in a man's shirt and leggings which she's wrung out. There's a big grin on her face.

I go to her and enfold her tightly in my arms again and we kiss and kiss. Sweet heavens, this is even more magical than I remembered. I can't get enough of her. She seems pleased to see me too. Finally she lays her cheek against my chest.

"You feel wonderful, and you're not dirty like I was when I arrived at the pond just now."

"I washed in the creek yesterday. I caught fish too. Do you want some?"

"Absolutely. I have cherries from your farm also."

I take the pack off my back and she brings hers over. We plop down on the small sandy beach and I remove my soaked boots. Handing her a large piece of fish, I note how thin she has become. "You've had a hard journey?"

She nods and between bites gives me the highlights. I reach into her bag and begin eating cherries, then hand her the last piece of fish and some dry bread. I am engrossed in her story. I admire the determination of my sheltered but spirited girl, who has persevered through her fears and hardships to arrive here. She expresses her gratitude that my Father sent her Mahujael, and that God has truly protected and guided her.

She finishes the dry bread, scooping up water in a metal cup to wash it down, then smiles at me, a truly radiant smile.

I ask, "Don't you want some cherries?"

"No, they're pretty much the first thing I ate in two days, and I'm afraid I ate too many this morning. I'm so grateful not to have to eat them for lunch and dinner. Thank you, Ham. Thank you for coming."

"You and Father were so silly not to tell me what was going on. I would have come sooner."

"I know. That's why I made him promise not to tell you. What if my papa had caught us together in Midgard, or anywhere else?"

"Well, I'm not leaving you again. After we foil your father's evil plan, we are going directly to the Ark."

Egyptus leans over and kisses me on the cheek, then laughs. "Well, okay, if you insist."

"I do."

EGYPTUS: I was afraid that I might never see Ham again. Now here he is and he even brought me food. We just need to determine if the Garden exists and life will be perfect.

I pull the Urn lid out of my pack. "Ham, I know that my papa and uncles are supposed to be about two days behind me, which probably means they'll get here tomorrow or the next day. The only clue I have to find the entrance to the Garden is written inside the Urn lid where the map to Eden was stored. See? It says:

'Bow to me from the East.
Wash before entering.
Ascend with a prayerful heart'."

Ham nods.

I continue, "Well, I've bowed and washed. Now I need to enter and ascend. Noah said there must be a hidden entrance."

Ham smirks. "Yes, there is." He looks down, trying to hide a guilty grin.

My eyes narrow. "Ham...what do you know about the entrance?"

"Well, I did grow up here, and my brothers and I swam in this pond a lot. In fact our Mother encouraged it, as it kept us bathed. Father would carve us little boats to bring here and sail. The water's warm, so we'd even come in winter, sometimes every day." He grins at me.

"And...you found the entrance?"

"Yes, it's behind the waterfall. Don't tell Father. We really couldn't help it. It's just there."

"And you went in?"

"Well, we were curious boys: Explorers, Adventurers. Okay, a little bit naughty. Shem went first. When he came back alive we all went in."

166

"What's the Garden like?"

"It's indescribably beautiful. Warm year round. Never rains or snows. We'd go up there and play every day we could in the winter. It's perfect. Want to see?"

Do I want to see the Garden of Eden? What a silly question. I'm on my feet instantly, stuffing my wrung-out clothes in my pack, which Ham takes from me. "What do we do with our stuff? What about Thor and Night?"

Ham pulls on his squishy boots. "Your father isn't due until tomorrow. Let's be safe and take the horses and leave them in the canyon while we stay in the Garden. When they arrive, the horses won't give us away."

He whistles for Thor. Night comes over also and bows so I can climb on. Ham watches. "Well, that's a new trick."

He jumps on Thor with both our packs on his back, our bedrolls and Mahujael's net tied in front. I follow him, feeling strangely unburdened without my pack and without the worry of needing to find the entrance to the Garden.

I tilt my head and watch him riding ahead of me. He rides like he's part of Thor: relaxed yet erect. The sun has streaked his hair even lighter blond than when I last saw him. It's longer too. And his skin is golden. He must have shaved this morning; his chin and jawline are crisp against his neck. I want to touch his face. I shake myself. Maybe later.

In the meantime, we're riding along the base of the mountain, which rises straight up. There are scattered wildflowers among the grasses. The sun is high now. Caressing. I breathe in deeply. It smells like warm earth and gladness.

Suddenly Thor turns right and disappears into the side of the mountain. I'm puzzled. Midnight can hear his sire, so follows him. We're in a narrow, short passageway, which soon opens up into a wider, grassy, slot canyon. Good hiding place. Ham dismounts and is over to help me off my horse before Midnight can bow. He says, "They'll be safe here. We may as well leave our stuff too."

"Won't we at least need the cherries?"

Ham chuckles. "It *is* a garden."

"There's food? Let's go!" I head for the entrance and notice a heavy, metal gate at the inside end of the passageway.

Ham goes to pat the horses and takes all the equipment and bridles off them. "You guys be good. We'll be back when we can." Thor nudges him, seeming unconcerned.

Night just seems happy with Thor's company. They are nonchalantly grazing when Ham joins me and shuts the gate behind us.

He takes my hand as we walk through the short passageway and out into the sun again. We retrace our horses' steps; Ham holding my hand, or putting his arm around my shoulders, like he wants to touch me to make sure that I'm really here with him. We don't hurry. I'm just so very happy to be with Ham again. Also I get to see the Garden, and both things together are giving me joyful butterflies in my stomach.

168

We speak of our journeys. He tells me about seeing the giant white bears and other animals from the north heading to the Ark, about Thor and the giants, seeing my father and uncles, and how Mahujael rescued him and told him not to mourn for or worry about him. God has been good to us all.

Chapter Eighteen

EGYPTUS: Soon enough, we're back at the pond. Mist and spray from the waterfall are blowing out across the water. Ham speaks above the noise of the falls. "You ready?" I nod.

We take our boots off to carry them, though Ham's are still damp from our greeting hug. He takes my hand and walks along the wall of the mountain until we're descending into the water. There's a ledge beneath our feet that continues behind the waterfall. We are waist deep.

Then Ham turns into a narrow slot slanted in the rock. This slot is just big enough for one person to slide through sideways, but I find it opens up wider after the entrance. The only light is coming through this narrow entry.

There are stairs winding up. Ham climbs and sits down a few steps up out of the water to pull on his boots. "You'll need your boots on. It's a rocky stairway. Be super careful."

I look up into the dark, invisible tunnel. "How far up is it?"

"Three thousand and sixteen steep stairs, give or take a thousand. We're going to the top of the mountain."

"You're kidding. And you used to do this on a daily basis?"

He smiles wryly, "You'll see why when we get to the top. It's worth it. Hey, we were kids. Lots of energy."

"Right." To the top. Worth it. I'm a little nervous.

"Okay, it's going to be very dark. Keep your right hand on the wall of the passageway. Feel each stair with the tip of your boot, then step up. They are quite uniform in height but a little rough. If you follow right behind me, you'll be able to hear my footsteps to guide you. We'll go slowly and stop to catch our breath every hundred stairs or so. We'll be fine."

"There aren't critters in here, are there?"

"No, at least there never were. You'll meet the talking rabbits at the top though."

He starts climbing. Talking rabbits. Right. Whatever. I follow him after pulling on my boots. The dim light is soon far below us, then gone altogether.

Ham stops for our first breather. I ask, "How long does it take to get to the top?"

"Not long when you're twelve, longer when you're ninety." He continues up. I follow.

About ten breathers later I say, "I never would have found that tiny entrance, and if I had, I wouldn't have dared go up a long, dark flight like this."

"Nope. The garden is actually very well protected. No one finds it, except maybe the soaring eagles, and three curious boys."

"My papa will come up if he finds the entrance. He's determined."

"Well, we'll be there. We'll outsmart him somehow."

I like that idea: intelligence wins over force.

We continue upward. My thighs and calves are starting to burn, but at least I've grown accustomed to the pitch black and feeling for each step in the dark. The stairs have twists and turns, but by keeping my hand on the wall I can tell when they're coming. A few rest stops later it feels like we've been ascending forever.

"Ham, I need to sit for a minute."

"Okay." He comes to sit, squeezing beside me on my narrow step, and puts his arm around my shoulder. His free hand strokes my neck, then slides up to my face, then he traces over my lips with his thumb. I turn my face to him and he kisses me. His lips are the warmest thing in the cool passageway. The blind darkness enhances the sensation of firm but yielding flesh sliding across my mouth. I feel my insides melting and pull away.

Ham chuckles and clears his throat. "I guess kissing must wait until after we save the world from devious would-be immortals."

"Well, okay," I reply.

We rise and ascend. An eternity later I say, "Hey, the lid said 'Ascend with prayer'."

"Oh, I've been praying this whole time."

"Yes, I'm praying my legs will make it. They're really burning and starting to shake."

Ham says, "I guess we'd better follow the lid's instructions exactly. Let's sit and have a vocal prayer." We sit and Ham's arm is around me again.

"Do you want to say it?" he asks.

"Sure."

I close my eyes in the darkness and say a short prayer of thanks. Afterward I feel better, having precisely fulfilled the lid's instructions.

We stand and begin climbing again. After a while Ham announces, "We're getting closer. Can you feel the change in the air?"

"I can. It is slightly warmer and fresher."

Soon the faintest light illuminates the tunnel from above. There will be no more rest stops. We're both energized and excited. Finally we're on the top step, breathing heavily. There's another slanted slot to step through to enter the garden.

"Wait," Ham puffs.

We stand for a minute, catching our breath and letting our eyes adjust. I can't believe I'm actually here with Ham entering the Garden of Eden.

Ham bends down and pulls off his boots then kneels and takes mine off too. "This is a sacred place. No shoes allowed. Plus, we don't need them here." He picks up the footwear.

"Okay we're ready," he says, and takes my hand. He leads me through the passage and I step out into filtered sunlight and catch my breath. I can't believe what lies before me.

The first impression is overwhelming color. Everything seems to be shimmering, radiating vibrant hues. There are giant trees creating a broken green canopy overhead, filtering rays of white-gold sunlight down between them. Shorter trees underneath the high canopy are full of colorful fruit. There are bushes laden with more fruit, interspersed with boulders and rocks placed perfectly, some in pools of water, others bordering patches of luxurious short grass for lounging or playing on.

And everywhere, everywhere there are flowers. Every color. I've never seen or breathed air this pure and clean. Drifts of fruit and flower scents come by me.

The air is warm. Not too warm, not chilly, just the perfect temperature for moving or sleeping. It's very quiet. I hear water running and the faint rustle of leaves. But no birds. Not even insects. Just us breathing.

Transfixed, I stand and absorb the scene for a long time. Finally I turn to Ham, who has been watching my reaction. "This is quite the play yard," I say.

"Yes, we had a lot of fun here. It is, of course, my favorite place from childhood. I suppose we should have brought Mother and Father here, but we knew he'd forbid us to ever come back. It was hard to move away from it. I guess the three of us felt like Adam being cast out.

"I suspect Shem and Japheth have brought their wives here. I've been back a few times since we moved away. It's a good place to think." He squeezes my hand. "And now I get to share it with you. Come, eat something. You'll feel better."

"We're allowed to eat?"

"Yes, everything except fruit from the two trees in the middle of the Garden. The Tree of Life, of course, and we were always too chicken to try the fruit of the Tree of Knowledge of Good and Evil, even though our bodies already suffer from the effects of it; I mean because Adam and Eve ate it, making all of us mortal."

I'm still a little dazed. Mortality. Of course. It began here. Ham stashes our boots behind a nearby bush.

I ask, "What's your favorite fruit?"

"All of it. Here, try this." He reaches up above us and plucks what looks like a peach and hands it to me. It is so beautiful -- peachy color blushed with rosy pink. Not a flaw. I sniff it. It's bursting with perfect peach fragrance.

"Here." Ham takes it from me, takes a bite, and hands it back, closing his eyes in pleasure. "Oh yeah. I'd forgotten."

I bite. Juice and flavor explode in my mouth, almost sending me to my knees with joy. It has a smooth but firm texture, less stringy than a mortal peach.

"Wow. We should take this and plant it wherever we end up living."

"We can't. There's no seed in it, or in any of the fruit. My brothers and I tried to take the fruit out many times, but by the time it gets to the bottom of the stairs it turns to dust."

"Curious. So if we eat all the peaches, they're gone forever?"

"Tomorrow there will be a flower where we picked this, and in a few days there will be a new peach in its place."

I take another bite. "You're right. I do feel better. Suddenly my legs feel great, and my stomach is no longer suffering the effects of the cherries."

"The fruit here will cure anything that's wrong with you. Mom never could believe how quickly we got over ailments. Once I fell off my horse and broke my leg. My brothers helped me up all those stairs. One bite and I took myself back down. We never did tell her I'd been hurt."

"No use stirring up trouble."

I have new respect for the fruit. Ham goes over to a bush, picks a purple berry and hands it to me. It's too pretty to eat, but I do anyway. Delicious. Sweet and tart at the same time. I'm sure this is heaven.

I follow him slowly through the Garden and we graze as we go. Soon I'm so full I can't eat any more. We've left a trail of half-eaten fruit behind us. Ham says the ground will absorb our litter by tomorrow. Charming. A little creepy, but charming.

We've walked quite a way into the garden. It's larger than I thought. Paths wind through it. We've crossed creeks several times on stepping stones. Ham knows his way around.

"Where are we going?"

"To the middle. To the Tree of Life."

Just hearing that sounds surreal. We're in no hurry and put our arms around each other as we saunter along.

Ham tells me about the games they played here -- a lot of hide and seek. Another where one would hide an object and the others would have to find it. There were many versions of that game. There were steeplechase races, tag games, and they'd climb the trees -- even the highest ones. If they fell and got hurt they'd just eat the fruit to heal. They brought their toy boats up here to sail and race in the warm ponds and streams, sometimes sending them over the eastern waterfall into the pond below.

All of them became excellent swordsmen, as they'd fight until someone was bruised or bleeding, stop for a healing snack, then fight on. "I'm sure this is where Shem became enamored with swords. He makes the finest to be found. We all carry one of his. And Japheth never stopped loving boats, large and small."

And there were always games with the rabbits and stories from the rabbits. Finally I ask, "What's a rabbit?"

"Oh, you'll meet them soon. They're probably just giving us some time alone. Believe me, they're not shy. Oh, here we are to the White Garden. We kept this off limits."

Sure enough, the White Garden lives up to its name. The many varieties of white flowers glow pristinely against their rich green leaves. The boulders and rocks are white. Even the paths are laid with white stone. It's all luminous.

In the middle is a low hillock on which grow two trees almost entwined, seemingly from the same gnarled roots. One of them has brilliant white glowing fruit, the other glowing gold fruit. They both sparkle in the sun from roots to branch tip. They are ethereal: the most beautiful things I've ever seen, besides Ham, of course.

From under the hillock they're perched on, water flows out in four directions, beginning the four rivers that Noah said originate at the mountain.

The stream flowing eastward becomes the waterfall that covers the entrance, then eventually grows to become the large Silver River in the Land of Nod, which I've followed here.

The White Garden is exquisite.

"Why did you keep it off limits?"

"That's the Tree of Life, the white-fruited one. It's the center of the garden. We didn't want to disturb it. I'm still terrified of those trees. Old habit, I guess."

"We can stay out of the white garden."

"No. We've got to figure out what to do about the fruit and your father and uncles." We clasp hands, step into the sun, and slowly walk toward the hillock. There are no overhead trees here. It is the brightest part of Eden. It feels extra special -- very sacred. I feel peaceful and happy inside. Ham looks at me and smiles. He appears peaceful and happy too. I smile back and say, "You are the most handsome thing in this garden."

He touches my lower lip and replies, "You have the sweetest fruit."

We arrive at the twin trees. Up close, they certainly are impressive. They don't even look real. They radiate like candles.

"What now?" I ask.

"I guess we could sit underneath them."

The hillock is covered by lush grass. Ham sits, then lays back and looks up at the fruit hanging off the trees. I do too. Ham is deep in thought. It is so quiet. I close my eyes.

Chapter Nineteen

HAM: The glowing fruit hangs above us: Eternal life. I look over at Egyptus. She's sound asleep curled on her side facing me, her arm pillowing her head. Probably Adam once lay here and watched Eve sleep.

He had such an easy life: eat, play, talk, love, sleep. I could live like that here with Egyptus and be exceedingly content. I think about that -- content forever. Never any challenges, never growing, never developing new talents, never having children, grandchildren.

I imagine having a baby with Egyptus. Our baby would be beautiful with her mother's lustrous dark skin and big eyes. I'd watch her learn to roll over, take her first steps, comfort her if she got sick. Hopefully she'd love music. We could play together.

Perhaps Adam thought about these things, about making a family with Eve. Maybe being eternally content wasn't enough. Maybe he wanted more.

It's just mid-afternoon, but it seems like it's been such a long day. I close my eyes too.

I awaken a little disoriented to the sound of tiny voices coming from near my feet. Egyptus' eyes are open too, but she hasn't moved.

"This one's Ham! I can tell by his toes. He has the longest toes."

"Look at this one! His toes are brown like me."

Egyptus looks like she wants to giggle.

"Shem said the Ark's getting done when he last visited. Do you think Ham has come to get us?"

"Oh, I do hope so, that would be so exciting!"

I roll my eyes at Egyptus, then sit up. At our feet are two small rabbits, one white, one brown. "Hello Fluffy, Filo. Very pleased to see you again. This is Egyptus."

The critters bow to her then say in unison, "Pleased to meet you Egyptus."

Filo, the brown one, turns to me. "She's a girl! Is she your wife?"

"She will be soon."

Fluffy offers, "Shem visited. He brought his wife to eat the fruit. She was sick. Then she was healed and they cried." Fluffy turns to Eyptus, "Are you sick?"

"No," Egyptus shakes her head. "So you're a rabbit? I've never seen a rabbit before."

"That's because when the other animals went to the mortal world we stayed here to guard the Garden, so we haven't reproduced yet."

I pipe in, "Tell Egypt why God chose you to stay."

"God said we'd be so good at reproducing that we could stay here if we wanted. But that we'd need to leave before the Garden was destroyed."

"He should have let the rats stay too," Egyptus opinions.

I smile. "Shem was right though. It's time for you to leave the Garden. This place will be washed away in a flood soon. You'll be left immortal and then you'll never get to reproduce. The world will be permanently Rabbitless."

Filo's tiny rabbit shoulders sag. "Well, we knew this day was coming. We won't be able to talk to you anymore, will we?"

"No, none of the animals out there speak Adamic. They speak their own languages though. You'll still be able to talk to each other. Someday, after we're all resurrected and become immortal, we'll all speak Adamic again. Then you can tell me stories about what happened to you in the world." The rabbits seem cheered by this promise.

I continue, "When Egyptus and I leave here, we're going directly to the Ark so we won't drown in the big storm. You can come with us and ride on Thor. Do you remember my stories about my horse Thor?"

"Yes," Fluffy says, "he's the biggest, bestest horse in the world."

"That's right," Egyptus agrees, managing to keep a straight face. "I've ridden on him. It was the best horseback ride I've ever had. Riding with Ham is awesome. He keeps you warm." Now I have to keep a straight face.

"Okay," Filo says. "Hand me down one of those fruits."

"You have to eat a fruit to become mortal?" I ask.

"Well, all the other animals did. They are the only fruit in the Garden to have seeds. I think that's what makes them dangerous to us immortals -- they can reproduce.

"Adam named everything in the garden, including us. After he bit the fruit and found the seeds, he named them cacao, which means happiness. The fruit is full of cacao. They're very delicious, I'm told. One of the most delicious fruits, next to the fruit of the Tree of Life, which everyone says is *the* most delicious, and I agree."

"That's right, you still eat the fruit of the Tree of Life. Listen, before you become mortal, we need your help with a problem. Three men, who are Egyptus' father and two uncles, are coming to the Garden. They want to eat the fruit of the Tree of Life and become immortal without repenting and following God's laws."

Fluffy cries, "Oh but they mustn't! They'll be unclean forever! Never able to wash their sins away through the Messiah's atonement and enter Heaven again."

"That's right. Plus they'd be able to do a lot of bad things in the world and no one could stop them. So we've got to think of a way to prevent them from becoming immortal. They can't eat the white fruit and they'll be here as soon as tomorrow."

"Fluffy and I could stand underneath the trees and tell them that the gold fruit is from the Tree of Life."

"No, they know it's the white fruit, or they'll figure it out. They have a map to lead them here. It has instructions on it."

"Fluffy and I could just kill them."

"No I don't want their blood on your paws. And it would upset Egyptus. She'd develop a fear of rabbits." Egyptus looks horrified and nods.

Fluffy offers, "You could block up the entrance. Throw rocks down the stairs."

"I think they'd just move them. Anyway, then *we* couldn't get out. What if we picked all the fruit from the Tree of Life and hid it?"

Fluffy says, "It grows back faster than the other fruits. It would probably grow back by morning."

"Then we'll pick it again."

"But what if they like it here and stay around? The fruit will grow back and they'll discover it."

Now my shoulders slump. "I don't know what to do. I don't even want to touch the fruit to pick it. What if the juice gets on me and turns me immortal?"

Filo shrugs, "Then you'd just have to eat the golden fruit. The cacao seeds would make you mortal again."

"So it's reversible?"

"Yes."

Egyptus inserts, "What if they ate both fruits at once?"

Filo responds, "I think the fruit and seeds of the Tree of Knowledge of Good an Evil would win. It's powerful. Even one lick causes mortality."

"That just might work," I say. "I guess we're going to have to try it. I'll cover the white fruit with juice from the gold fruit."

Egyptus looks worried. "You mean actually eat it?"

"Yes, I'll do it."

"No, I will. He is *my* murderous father after all."

"I won't risk your soul."

"I thought of the idea."

I reach for Egyptus and gather her warm body in my arms. I hold her there a minute then kiss the top of her head. "All my life these two trees with their fruits have terrified me. Let me prove that my love for you overrides all fear."

Egyptus nods and kisses me on the cheek. "Okay. According to Filo it is reversible, after all."

Filo pipes up, "Yes, but once the gold fruit's inside you, you'd have to wait a while before you could switch back to being immortal with the white fruit. It would have to work its way out of your body until there wasn't a trace left."

I look at him quizzically. "Filo, you seem very well informed about this."

"I've been here a long time. One animal tried to eat the white fruit after eating the gold fruit but he didn't change back."

Fluffy shivers, "Yes, it was the horrid snake. Thank goodness he got thrown out of here."

I nod. "This is really good news. If we can taint the fruit and trick them, they'll leave the garden not knowing that if they waited a few days or weeks or months, however long it would take, they could try again. Let's try desecrating a fruit."

The others watch as I stand up and grab a golden fruit and tug. It lies glowing in my palm. So beautiful. It's large enough to fill my whole hand. Oval shaped, with deep groves running from top to bottom like stripes. I split it open with my thumbs. Sure enough, the inside is lined with large, juicy, golden brown seeds. It smells great. I wouldn't mind eating this at all. I go over to the white tree and take the two golden halves and rub it all over a fruit. Then I do a second fruit, then all of the fruits on that branch.

"Let it dry," Egyptus says before I can pick a white fruit and eat it. "It will be dry when the men come. We need to see if even the dried juice is effective."

"Good idea." I throw the golden fruit down and go to wash in the stream trickling from under the hillock. I don't want any juice to get in me from off my hands, messing up the trial results.

The sky is getting dark. The candescent fruit lights up the White Garden even at night. It's lovely.

I go sit by Egyptus. We cuddle together and Filo and Fluffy launch into stories about how Adam and Eve would play tricks on each other. How when all the other animals were there, it was a busy place and they'd have contests and make up stories and put on plays. How Eve's best friend besides Adam was a female orangutan, and Adam's was a large yellow dog.

Finally I stand and go pick a defiled white fruit. I sit down by Egyptus. My hand is shaking a little. The fruit is so beautiful -- radiating the purest light. Lit up like the energy of life itself. It's shaped like a big, fat pear, and is firm and quite heavy in my hand. It smells divine -- like vanilla and sugar and cream and the cacao fruit I rubbed it with. The other three are watching me closely. I put it to my mouth and take a bite. Oh my. It *is* the most delicious fruit in the universe. I could eat the whole tree. I sit quietly, feeling for any changes. For a second I do feel lighter and extraordinarily happy, then I feel normal again in the next heartbeat.

"I think it worked," I say. The other three let out a sigh of relief. "I'm still mortal."

Fluffy comes to put a paw on my wrist. "Your heart is beating. An immortal's heart, like ours, has no need to beat. There's no blood of life in our bodies." I nod.

"You'd better finish that fruit," Egyptus says. "I know my father and uncles will eat the whole thing. They'll probably eat all they can."

I gladly finish it. Then I go rub the juice from a gold fruit on every white fruit left on the tree. I plan on repeating that dousing every morning and night until they arrive. Hopefully they'll come soon. We need to get going to the Ark.

Chapter Twenty

NEHOR: The sun is setting as Mesael, Nabal, and I arrive at Eden Mountain, two days after leaving the border of the Blue Hills. Our progress has been slow and hampered by Mesael's illness. He's never recovered from his alcoholic stupor. Mostly I'd just like to leave him behind.

I'd kind of like to leave Nabal behind too. I've realized that once we eat the fruit, the three of us are going to be stuck together forever, and I'm having difficulty remembering why I needed them. Surely I can get along without Mesael's creative genius or Nabal's foresight and financial abilities, can't I?

We approach the east side of the mountain and its lacy waterfall. According to the map, the entrance is directly behind the falls.

We pull up at the small pond at the base of the falls. It would be really nice to have a bath. Gratefully I slide off my horse. Nabal does the same.

We help Mesael off his mount. He's so weak I don't know how he's stayed on all day, and he collapses to the ground. Nabal and I look at each other, then he shrugs and goes to get our brother's gear off his horse. He unrolls Mesael's blanket and covers him up, then puts his pack under his head for a pillow.

I walk around the pond, touch the side of the mountain, and look over at the waterfall. I slip off my boots, then inch out into the water, with my back against the mountain's wall. There's rock beneath my feet that I follow until I'm behind the falls. I find the narrow, practically invisible crevice, the entry to the Garden of Eden. I feel the first excitement that I've felt in days, but am too weary to climb a mountain right now.

I inch back along the rock ledge until I'm on the beach again. I'm wet to my waist. Walking back to Nabal I say, "It's there." He nods.

We gather wood from the clumps of trees, build a small fire by our sleeping brother, and sit by it. I bring out all the jerky and dried fruit we have left. After we eat the white fruit tomorrow we will never be hungry again. What immortal eats for anything but pleasure? Nabal and I lie down, pull our coats over us, and fall asleep.

190

I awaken to the sound of the waterfall and the sun warming my body. My legs continue damp from entering the pond last night, so it feels good. I sit up and see Nabal beside Mesael, who is still lying down. Nabal seems very still. No, his shoulders are shaking. Is he crying? I look at Mesael. He's very, very still. Not breathing. He's dead. I sit back and put my head in my hands.

'Oh Mesael, why did you have to be so careless? Why did you choose intoxication and carousing over immortality?' I hear screaming and wailing. I'm on my feet. It's me screaming and wailing. I'm kicking Mesael's lifeless body. "I hate you! I hate you!" I'm screaming. "How could you do this to us? Why? Why? Why?" I collapse sobbing on the ground. "You're so stupid! I hate you!" I lay for a while, crying and gasping for air. Finally I'm quiet. I don't ever want to move again.

A long time, a very long time later, Nabal comes over to jab my shoulder with his boot. "Get up," he says. "Help me drag his body to his grave."

I stir. I don't want to, but I sit up, then stand and join Nabal. Mesael looks terrible. His face is mottled, his body stiff. He must have vomited blood before dying, because it is everywhere, dried and caked on his face, clothing and hair. I turn where I stand and wretch bile on the ground. Then wiping my mouth with the back of my sleeve, I look at Nabal and say, "Let's do this."

We both grab one of Mesael's legs and drag him toward the trees where Nabal has dug the grave. Considering his lack of tools, it's quite a deep hole. I would be up to my chest if I stood in it. We dump Mesael in and begin to move the mounded earth back into the grave over his body. It takes a while. The sun creeps lower in the sky.

When we're done there's just a heap of earth. I'm a sweaty, dirty mess. So is Nabal. "Let's swim," I say.

Listlessly we walk to the pond and take off our stinky clothes. Here I am, the king of the greatest tribe on earth, and at the moment I'm completely destitute. Naked. Hungry. Dead brother. Tomorrow things will change. I vow that I will become immortal, that I will live in the finest palace, that I will leave my feelings for my dead wife, Egyptus' mother, behind me, and replace her with one queen after another. The world will worship me. They will have to. I will make them.

I dive into the pond and swim back and forth. Going under the waterfall I surface behind it and squeeze through the slot that is the entry to Eden. "I'm coming!" I scream up the black tunnel. "I'm coming tomorrow, so be ready! Nothing's going to stop me!"

I retreat back across the pond and see that Nabal has another fire burning. He's going through Mesael's things, tossing them in, watching them burn. His bloody blanket is currently being consumed. Each mourns in his own way, I suppose.

I walk up to him and pick up my dusty clothes. "We'll go to Eden in the morning."

He lies down by the fire and rolls away from me. "I'm going to sleep now. I'll be ready."

There's nothing to do but watch the stars come out. Eventually I'm asleep too.

Morning brings a new feeling – hope. And hunger. We didn't eat yesterday. I look around. Nabal is over in the nearby field with the three horses. I walk over to him. He says, "Maybe we should eat one of them."

"That sounds like a lot of trouble and we'd have to stop and prepare the meat and cook it. Let's see if we find Eden through the passageway. If we don't, we'll come back and eat a horse."

Nabal smirks. "I'm hungry enough to eat a horse."

I smack him playfully on the shoulder. "Let's go find immortality."

We head back around the pond, leaving our belongings strewn on the beach. Wading onto the rock ledge until we're behind the waterfall, we enter the slot in the rock, Nabal painfully squeaking his stocky body through.

Our feet find steps underwater in the back of the slot and we stumble up them to dryness. We go up until the faint light below us almost disappears.

Nabal pauses behind me. "Nehor, are you sure this is the way?"

"No, I'm not sure of anything anymore, but I figure we don't have much to lose. I'm going all the way up. Turn back if you want. I'll let you know how it turns out."

I begin climbing again. Nabal continues behind me. It is pitch black. The only sound is our labored breathing. It's cool here in the mountain's bowel, but I feel and smell the sweat coming off myself. The climb is miserable and seemingly never-ending. After a while our hands and shins are bloodied from tripping on the uneven, sharp steps. I begin wondering if I'm insane; if we're really going up, or if it's just a cruel illusion.

"Nehor, I can't go on," I hear from below me. I stop and feel my way back to Nabal. He's whimpering, breathing too quickly. "It feels like the stone walls are squeezing me. I can't breathe."

"Listen," I say, shaking him, "I lost my favorite wife, and now Mesael. I'm not going to lose you too. Get yourself together. Take some deep breaths. We're going to finish these steps, eat the fruit, jump down the side of the mountain if we have to, go back to my daughter Egyptus, who hopefully is holding things together at home, and rule the world. Got it?"

I feel anger building in me. Anger added to my determination that this whole nightmare is going to end. I'll make it end. I feel Nabal nod, take a deep breath, and we climb again.

Finally, after what seems like hours, when our limbs feel like burning jelly and we are climbing so slowly it almost doesn't seem to count, finally there is the faintest light from above. We can't seem to move any faster, but there is hope.

Another eternity later I scale the top step. There's a narrow exit in front of me leading to light. I fall through the slot, exhausted, and land on soft ground. It is so bright I cover my eyes. I hear Nabal land beside me and gasp.

Chapter Twenty-one

NABAL: I open my eyes and blink. Wow. Color everywhere. Fantastic. So quiet and peaceful, yet so alive and shimmering. When I rule the world I'm going to come build my palace here.

We lay there breathing heavily, taking in the loveliness, the serenity, when a little voice firmly says, "Hello." We jump. A small brown creature is standing on its haunches in front of us. It looks like a rounded cat, but has long ears. And it talks.

"Who are you?" it demands.

I gather my wits. "Um, I am Nehor, and this is my brother Nabal."

"You're brown like me. Are any more of you coming today?"

"No. There's just two of us now."

The creature cocks its head. "This is sacred ground. Take off your boots, and your swords and knives."

Nabal and I comply. Boy, our boots stink, and they're still damp.

Nabal politely asks, "And may we inquire who you are?"

"I am Filo the rabbit. I am the guardian of the Garden of Eden."

I stare open-mouthed at the tiny creature and say, "I was expecting Cherubim and a flaming sword as guardian."

"Yes, that's me," the rabbit says. He points to his rounded tummy. "Cherubim." He indicates then wiggles his sword-shaped ears. "Flaming swords. I'm immortal, you're not. If I wanted to, I could tear you both into tiny pieces and let the garden absorb you." Somehow, I believe him.

"Why are you here?" he demands.

I reply, "We have come to see if the legends are true, if the Garden exists."

"Well, here it is. You can leave now."

Nabal pipes up, "Wait, please, kind rabbit. We desire to see the Tree of Knowledge of Good and Evil, which our first parents ate from, causing them to become mortal."

"Why?"

"We long to witness to the world of its existence. So many are unbelievers now."

"Hmmm..." the rabbit is thinking. "I suppose you want to see the Tree of Life too?"

"If it is convenient." Nabal really is good at this.

The rabbit puts his tiny paws on his tiny round hips and paces back and forth. "Okay, but you mustn't touch or eat any of the fruit that grows anywhere in the Garden."

"Of course we won't."

"If you did, you'd be putting your eternal souls in danger, you realize that?"

"Do enlighten us, good sir."

"Your spirit inside you is already immortal. The plan is for your body to die then resurrect to become immortal too."

"How can that happen?"

"A Messiah will be born. His life and sacrificial death will make it possible for all those who live and die on this earth to have immortality, and possibly achieve eternal life. You see, all those who die will resurrect and have an immortal body. But those who repent and do their very best to follow God's commandments will also have eternal life -- which is living with God again.

Those not living with God will live in various degrees of hell, which will vary from a beautiful place just outside his kingdom, all the way down to being eternally stuck with the devil and his angels, who will never have immortal bodies because they refused to come to earth and get one in the first place."

Nabal says, "So our brother Mesael will already become immortal just by being born and dying."

"That's right."

I add, "And my dead wife Egyptus will not only become immortal, but she will have eternal life also because she always repented of her mistakes and always tried to do what God said."

198

"That's right."

I give a shrug. "Agreed then, no eating the fruit."

"Follow me." Filo begins hopping down a winding path. We stand to follow. "Don't touch anything. I'll take you straight to the two trees."

I trail right behind Nabal, who is closely following the little creature. He's really very cute. I'll let him be my pet once I rule the world.

Nabal and I both stumble once in a while since our attention is on the Garden around us, not the path under our feet. I practically land face down in a stream when I miss the stepping stones.

Filo looks back at us and sighs. "We can walk slower if you want."

"No, no," I say. "Carry on."

A few more twists and turns and suddenly we're surrounded by light and all the flowers are white. It's almost blinding.

"Here are the sacred trees," Filo states. He's standing on a wide mound. Above him are the two most extraordinary trees. Their trunks and branches twist and bend like two frozen dancers. They seem to grow from the same tortured roots. They look like they love each other, like they belong together. One has brilliant white fruit, the other brilliant gold. Their leaves sparkle and twinkle as they move in the breeze.

"Oh my goodness," Nabal mutters. He collapses to his knees. "It's all true."

I turn to Filo and bow. "Thank you, kind and noble guardian. May we have a moment to contemplate the goodness, grace, and mercy of God as expressed in these two trees before we leave?"

"Yes, of course," says Filo. And hopping over the other side of the mound, he disappears.

I rush over to Nabal who is still kneeling, staring at the glorious sight in front of him. He looks transported. I know how he feels.

"Nabal, we did it! The one with the white fruit is the tree of life." I run over and pluck two firm, glowing white fruits and run back to Nabal to hand him one. He looks horrified and stands up.

"What are you doing?" he cries.

"I'm going to eat this. Quick, take this one, it's yours."

"No!" he shouts, and backs away. "I don't want immortality like this. I don't want to be damned. I want to see God again."

I am enraged. "Well, I want it now!"

I bite into the radiant fruit. It tastes so good, so juicy, I'm halted in my chewing, just so I can savor it. So, so good. Then I feel it singing in my veins.

I look down at my hands. The cuts and scratches are disappearing. My shins are whole again too. I feel wonderful! My heart is beating strongly. I'm immortal!

"Yes!" I yell. Letting out a whoop I jump around, my hands in the air still clutching the fruits. Nabal is staring at me. He looks terrified. With my new strength I run and knock him flat on his back. Landing on top of him, I shove a fruit into his mouth. Some of the juice gets in because he stops struggling.

"Tastes good, doesn't it? Look, your scratches are healed. And now I'm not the only damned one. Guess I like having a brother after all."

He grumbles, "If you really liked me, you wouldn't have committed me to eternal hell."

I stand up, then pull him to his feet. "You'll get over it. Let's go before that rabbit comes back." We start walking toward the entrance, but are soon lost. The paths all twist and turn like a maze. Since we're breaking all the rules, we eat fruit off every bush and tree we pass. Some seem similar to the fruits and berries we've already eaten in the world, some seem brand new. They're all delicious, of course.

We load our pockets for later. Finally I look up. "See, Nabal? The sun is setting, so that's the west. We came in the east, so the exit is that way." With our backs to the sun, we troop to the east, sometimes staying on paths, sometimes trampling through clearings, bushes, flowers, and over rocks.

Finally we spot our boots and weapons lying where we took them off.

"Here we are!" I exclaim. We sit to pull them on.

Nabal wistfully says, "I wish I could stay here forever."

"I don't," I reply. "I don't feel comfortable here. This place feels too...good. It gives me the chills."

"Yes," Nabal looks around. "Good...sacred."

I head through the narrow exit and Nabal reluctantly follows behind.

Chapter Twenty-two

HAM: Egyptus and I have watched Nehor and Nabal's trip through the Garden from our vantage point high in the canopy of a tree. Egyptus wept quietly while watching her father's behavior. After they leave I whisper, "Are you okay?"

"Not yet," she replies. "It's going to take some time for me to accept that power is so important to papa that he'd do anything, however evil, for it. But, painful though it is, I love him. He is my father, and part of my heart. And now I'll never see him again. I feel like the world has already ended in a way."

I reach out from my branch and squeeze her hand.

After a few minutes she looks over at me and nods. We climb down. The rabbits meet us at the bottom. Fluffy is jumping up and down. "It worked! It worked!" We're all smiles, even Egypt.

"Filo, that was a masterful job," I say.

Egypt rejoices, "You converted Uncle Nabal. He wants to live with God again. Thank you."

"You're welcome," Filo replies. "Are we leaving now too?"

I reply, "It's getting dark now, so let's wait until morning. We need to give those two time to leave the area. Don't want to run into them."

"Good idea. Come, Fluffy, let's eat." They hop away for their last dinner here in Eden. Egypt and I wander with our arms around each other, visiting our favorite fruits. They are all so tasty.

We haven't kissed since we were climbing the stairs. I would like to remember kissing her here in Eden. We stop under an apple tree near the white garden. It's too dark now, but during the day you can see that it produces apples of different colors and flavors all on one tree. It's my favorite. On one visit when I was young I took a bite out of every apple on the tree.

I face Egypt. The glow from the white garden is enough to reveal her beautiful face. I'm hungry, but not for apples. I want to taste every part of *her*.

I don't touch her, deciding which delicious bit to begin with.

Her eyes are warm and trusting as she looks up at me.

She's Radiant. Lovely.

Finally I gently caress her right cheekbone, then lean and lightly kiss where I touched.

Enchanting.

She smiles at me, liking this new game.

I trace her left cheek, then leave a tiny kiss on its arc.

So perfect.

She closes her eyes, yielding, as yearning deepens within me.

I slowly sweep each sensitive eyelid, then brush across her long lashes and lids with my lips.

Oh bliss.

Our breathing accelerates.

Slowly, tenderly, I stroke the pad of my finger lightly across her forehead, then press my lips to its smoothness.

My cherished beloved.

Leisurely I touch the tip of her straight nose, then leave a butterfly kiss on it.

Divine.

She trembles slightly.

I reverently cup each side of her face, tilting it up. Skimming down her jaw line with both thumbs, I arrive at the slight cleft in her chin, and land a delicate kiss in the enchanting dent.

So dear.

I rest my forehead against hers, slowing my breathing, basking in the flickering intimacy.

Irresistibly drawn, my fingers alight on her right earlobe, gently caressing the center, then around the sensitive edge.

Bending down, I find it with my lips.

Oh so sweet. Sweet like happiness.

She tilts her head, offering me her left ear.

I stroke it so lightly, I can feel its invisible, soft down. I lean near, letting my warm breath touch her neck, inhaling her fragrance.

Heavenly sugar.

The appealing lobe receives one adoring, lingering kiss.

Exquisite, exquisite pleasure.

My insides are splintering into splendid shards: an ache that rejoices.

"Egyptus." She languidly opens her eyes.

Looking deep into her pure soul, I worshipfully vow: "I love you eternally and forever, and I desperately crave you. For that reason, after one last kiss, I promise I won't kiss you again until we get to the Ark."

Our gaze doesn't break.

She nods, accepting my pledge.

I trace her lower lip with my slightly quivering finger. Then circle up past the corner of her gorgeous, full lips and slowly outline the top edge, pausing to revel in the gratifying dip in the middle. I continue to the other corner, then stroke back and forth along her lower lip.

I smile and gather her fully, closely in my arms.

I feel her vibrant heartbeat underneath her silky skin.

Her aroma is delectable.

So warm against me.

All girl.

Nectar.

Slowly, slowly I bend my lips to hers.

They touch.

The contact is so heated and delicious, it's a shock. Like sunshine pouring through me. Warmth penetrates through all my layers, melting my core.

I'm full, I'm empty, I'm everything at once.

One kiss -- that's what I promised.

One long, luscious kiss.

Brilliant, joyous rapture.

I finally lift my lips and look into her eyes.

We breathe together, quickly, fervently, needing to cool the heat within. Still embracing, she rests her cheek on my chest. I stroke her hair, calming us both.

After a respite she asks, "So we're leaving for the Ark in the morning?"

I nod.

"And how long 'til we get there?"

"Too long."

We part. I don't touch her again. I don't dare. We lay on the grass and enjoy the twinkling stars and playfully argue about names for the many children that we hope to have. And grandchildren. And their children. Until we imagine there's a member of our family for each glittering star in the velvety dark sky above us.

EGYPTUS: The morning sunshine finds the four of us sitting under the sacred trees. It's time to go. Filo and Fluffy are on Ham's lap. He's petting their bellies and scratching them behind their ears. They love it. I fully understand why.

Ham says, "Well little pals, once you eat the fruit you won't be able to communicate with us. You'll be wild rabbits. But you'll feel the pull of the Ark, and we'll be headed toward it, so you should be content to travel with us, I hope."

Filo declares, "We love and trust you. We'll try to be good."

Ham has tears in his eyes and a catch in his voice. "I love you too. You've both been so good to my brothers and me. Such good examples." His voice breaks. "Our furry little mentors." He gives a wet laugh. "All the stories. So much fun."

Filo gives Ham's hand a little pat. "We loved playing with you three young boys. We let you in the Garden because we knew that we could trust you, and now I know that God led you back here to take us to the Ark, not just to stop the men from becoming immortal. Fluffy and I could have taken care of them ourselves if we'd had to."

"I'm sorry we caused you so much trouble," I say.

"No trouble. I do hope your father repents before the flood."

"I doubt he will, though he's a good man in so many ways."

Filo gives a little nod. "Mortals all have flaws. The trick is to acknowledge them and not let them keep you out of heaven."

I slowly nod. "This trip has taught me to trust the goodness of God, and His plan. I now resolve to appreciate what I have, instead of mourning all I have lost and will lose."

Fluffy hops over onto my lap. "It was lovely to meet you, Egyptus."

Now my eyes are wet. "Oh, Fluffy, I've only been here four days, but it seems I've always known you."

She tilts her head. "That's how friends are."

I smile at that. "I suppose so."

Fluffy requests, "Hand me a fruit please, Ham."

He leans up and plucks a golden fruit and sets it on the ground in front of her. Fluffy doesn't hesitate. She takes a bite -- one tiny little notch out of the side. She looks around for a minute, then hunches down, breathing fast.

We look at Filo, who shrugs. "Let the adventure begin." Then there is a second notch in the fruit and another rabbit hunched with the first.

Ham and I look at them. He sniffs. I reach over and give him a hug of comfort. He's still gathering his emotions when Fluffy starts hopping away and Filo follows.

"Um, Ham, we'd better get them before they escape."

Ham looks up. "Oh, of course. It looks like they're headed to the entrance." He stands and catches up with them and scoops both to his chest, where they seem content.

I hold on to his arm and we all walk toward the entrance. Once there, I stop and find my boots behind the bushes and pull them on. Then I hold our furry friends while Ham does the same.

One last look at the Garden, so beautiful, fresh, and empty now, and we are gone.

Chapter Twenty-three

NEHOR: "I am hungry."

    "Me too," agrees Nabal.

    "I didn't think immortals got hungry."

    "I guess we do."

    It is evening. We are halfway back to the blue hills. The horses are getting tired; we'll have to stop for the night. Apparently immortals sleep too, because we slept soundly on the beach all last night after the hellishly dark descent from the Garden.

HAM: We travel into the evening, both of us on Thor, with the rabbits tucked into a sheepskin nest in the leather pack on my back. When we arrived at the canyon at midday the gate was closed but only Thor was inside, still contentedly getting his fill of the grass. Midnight had apparently leaped over the tall gate, because he was nowhere to be found. We can travel more quickly together on Thor alone anyway.

We are crossing the ring of hills which divides Eden Valley from the plain. As we begin to descend the hill, we hear a loud rumble and the earth begins to shake. Thor stops and maintains his footing so we don't slide down the hill. The shaking continues. I wrap my arms around Egyptus and she hangs on Thor's mane. The trembling finally slows.

"What was that?" Egyptus sounds terrified.

"An earthquake." Behind us another ominous rumble begins. "Let's get out of here!"

Thor takes off down the hill, sensing a powerful danger. He doesn't slow at the bottom, but continues at full speed across the plain. No horse could possibly run faster. There's a deafening explosion behind us. My ears are ringing. I was wrong. Thor is running even faster. Hot wind and black dust surround us. We no longer have to worry about the garden being flooded. It just erupted into ash and smoke.

NEHOR: "Are you okay?" I yell.

"I think so," Nabal calls out. We are picking ourselves up off the ground after the shaking. "What happened?"

We hear a loud explosion and look toward Eden Mountain, which is still visible on the horizon. A large plume of smoke is rising from the center of the cone.

"Guess we're the last of the immortals."

HAM: We're heading almost directly south, staying a good distance away from the Kingdom of the giants. In two days I expect we'll leave the Eden plain, and arrive in the southern kingdom of Ethiopia. It can't happen too soon. Thor and the rabbits are surviving nicely on grass, but Egyptus and I need to buy some food. We're subsisting on shriveling cherries and dry bread for now. Ash from the new volcano still drifts down around us.

NEHOR: As we enter the Misty Blue Hills, the sound of drums begins. No matter. Nothing can hurt us, but we really need food. We're following the path along the Pison River through the hills. It will lead us back to Midgard. The king will feed us.

It's surprisingly hot today. The shade feels good. We travel single file on the narrow path. I'm riding Ahab. Nabal is behind me on Granger. Firelight was left behind in Eden valley.

It's so quiet. The drums have stopped. I hear only the stream and the horse's hooves. Now a new sound, the low growl of lions. The horses spook and take off running. I bounce around on Ahab, hearing screams behind me -- Horse? Man? Both? Ahab continues to bolt. It seems forever before I can stop him. I look back. No one is there. No one is anywhere. I know Nabal is okay. He's immortal, right?

I nudge Ahab around. He doesn't want to go back to the lions. He's going anyway. We trot back and find Granger on the ground. Dying, bloodied and ripped. Ugh. No Nabal. Wait, there's his boot. And his bloodstained coat -- ripped pieces of it anyway.

I follow the trail until I see what's left of Nabal, surrounded by lions. My furious roar terrifies the beasts and they scatter. Looking at Nabal's bones and flesh, I don't know what makes me more incensed -- that they've killed my brother, or that I'm not immortal after all.

I turn away and ride to Midgard.

EGYPTUS: I'm tired and sore, but at least I'll no longer be hungry. We crossed the River Gihon into Ethiopia this morning. After looking at Eden Plain's endless expanse of ash-strewn grass for so long, that's still what I see when I close my eyes.

We buy food at the first farm we come to: goat cheese and bread. After eating the exquisite fruit in Eden, I thought I'd not enjoy mortal food again, but I do. I enjoy it so, so much.

There's also a pile of baby carrots and new lettuce to share with Thor, Filo, and Fluffy.

We sit outside the farmhouse to eat so we can keep an eye on the rabbits, who apparently enjoy carrots and lettuce. The farmer is a muscular woman with light brown hair, dressed like me in a man's tunic and pants. She sits on the ground with us in the shade of a tree, glad to have the company.

Ham asks for news. She says that the earthquake damaged her house. She always knew the nearby plain of Eden was cursed. At least after the initial plume of smoke, the ash has stopped falling.

Then she says it's been warmer than usual and hasn't rained.

"Not at all?"

"No, not since the spring solstice celebration. I'm starting to irrigate the crops from a creek, since there's no rain. And a herd of strange horses was seen going east."

"What kind of horses were they?" Ham's always interested in the equine.

"All kinds. Horses with black and white stripes. Tall, long-necked horses with brown spots. Tiny horses with curved horns. Big, fat wrinkly grey ones with huge floppy ears and long noses that touched the ground."

"Horses? How long ago?"

"Probably been two or three weeks, maybe four. It was south of here. I didn't see them, but many did."

Ham and I look at each other. We're going to be too late. If it was four weeks ago, they might almost be to the Ark by now. We thank the kind farmer for her hospitality, invite her to come with us to the Ark; and when she declines, the four of us are back on Thor, urgently heading east.

NEHOR: Vanir is still upset over Ham's escape and Thor's loss. Upset and embarrassed. I'm still upset about Nabal and our failure at immortality.

We're eating alone at the table in Vanir's tent. No feasting tonight. Silence. Chewing. Finally to break the stillness I say, "I heard there was a little old man who was caught when Ham escaped. What did you do with him?"

"Mahujael? I sent him into the woods. Let the lions eat him and his stupid mule."

I wince at the thought of lions then stop. "Wait. What did you say his name was?"

"Mahujael. He came north with Ragnar the Chief and the men from Idum. They don't know what happened to his grandson who arrived with him. Everyone is keeping an eye out for the young man. I want to feed him to the lions too."

Vanir is drumming his fingers on the table. Something is bothering me about this story.

"What did this Mahujael look like? My brothers and I left for Eden the day Ham escaped, before your hunters had brought the old man to you. I assume he was light-skinned like Ham."

"No. Very dark skin, very old. Very small. Ragnar the Chief said he was from Nod."

No no no. It can't be. I jump up from the table to pace. My world is collapsing. Ham escaped to Eden. We went to Eden. It's a very large place, but still, few go there.

I know my great great grandfather Mahujael must be dead. He disappeared centuries ago after his father was murdered on the throne by Lamech, the same Lamech who later invaded Shum.

But what if he's not dead? He was a believer, allegedly in league with that fool Enoch, Noah's great grandfather. If he knew we were going to the Garden of Eden, he'd surely try to stop us.

But how would he find out? No one was there when the urn broke but myself, my brothers, and the dancing girls, who'd all been dismissed once I'd picked up the map from the urn pieces.

I sit down at the table and put my head in my hands. Think. Think. Think. Something doesn't make sense. I look up at Vanir, who is watching me like I'm crazy. "What did the grandson look like?"

"Oh, Ragnar gave us a good description. We sent it out on the drums. He's a Caananite, not quite as tall as you, slender, and almost too handsome. Long braided hair. Young -- in his first century."

Fear grips my chest, but I must ask, "Was he riding a horse?"

"Yes, Ragnar said it was a beautiful beast. All black. Large, but not as big as Thor. Well-trained. Named Night."

Oh my...no, no, no. It was Midnight. And the 'young man' had to have been Egyptus. I feel sick and hold my head in my hands again. Maybe she was meeting Ham in Eden Valley, the one place where it would be safe because no one goes there. They must have eloped and tried to hide from me. According to the giants, Ham grew up there. I knew Egyptus liked Ham, but I didn't think she'd do this to me. She's the one person I have left whom I love and trust.

Unless...no, it's unthinkable. Egyptus is a believer like her mother. If she knew I had the map, would she try to stop me? She did pick up the Urn pieces. Maybe she overheard something or just figured it out.

I feel empty inside. No, Egyptus wouldn't betray me.

But wait, Noah is trying to gather everyone to his Ark. He wouldn't let Ham settle in Eden Valley if he believed that it would be flooded.

That means there could only be one reason for them to go to Eden. They were following us. Somehow, they must have stopped us from becoming immortal. Now that we're gone, they'll head to the Ark.

Anger fills up the empty place inside me. I look up at Vanir. "I think I know where Thor is."

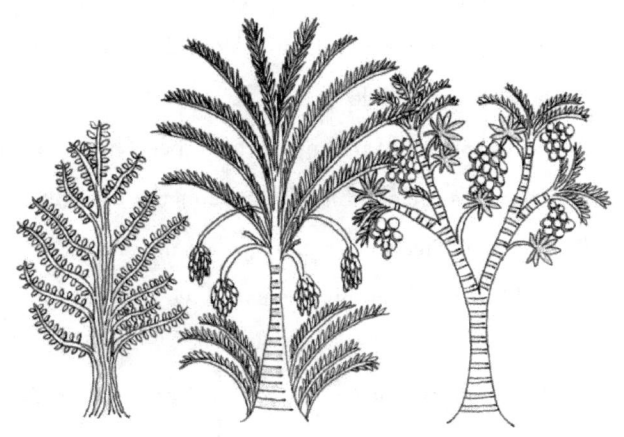

Chapter Twenty-four

EGYPTUS: Heat, heat, and more heat. I wear my red and gold scarf around my head to soak up sweat and protect my scalp from the sun. We've added ventilation holes to Ham's pack. The rabbits need relief from the heat. Ham's bedroll is smaller each day, as he cuts off a piece of it every morning to give the rabbits' pack a fresh lining.

We've traded all our non-essential items for food, as we need to travel as lightly and swiftly as possible. We even cut Mahujael's net smaller, just keeping enough to form a little cage to put over the rabbits at night. I kept a stone from its edge as a remembrance of my beloved grandpapa.

Every time we cross a stream or river we soak in it, drink our fill, and replenish our waterskins. We ride in wet clothes on a wet horse whenever possible.

The people of Hannanihah have been happy to sell us food, though prices are climbing because of the drought. We feel blessed to have whatever we can get. Ham is still carrying a fortune in gold from selling his horses, so we should be okay until we get to the Ark.

Many people recognize Ham from his trading and singing. He's famous. But he doesn't take time to perform on this trip. We just keep riding.

Strangely, no one joins us, though most have seen or heard about the strange animals heading east, which was the sign Noah warned of, and Ham reminds them about.

NEHOR: I'm across Havilah and now passing through Sharon. If there were any men left in this kingdom, they would kill me for betraying their dead king. As it is, I avoid the inhabitants as much as possible, stealing or buying food at outlying farms and sleeping in the open.

I feel like Ahab and the Silver River are my only friends. They're both taking me home to Nod, where I have army to gather.

HAM: Weeks have passed, and Egyptus hasn't complained yet. She really is doing well for a palace princess. If it weren't for the fact that we're racing against an impending flood, I'd be thoroughly enjoying this trip; I have her riding in front of me in my arms from before first light to full night.

We trade stories from our lives up until now, as well as our thoughts and opinions, and are getting to know each other very well.

I make up songs on demand for her entertainment. She makes up riddles I can never seem to solve.

Generally we try not to sit too closely on Thor, because it's too hot and our bodies stick together with sweat, but Egyptus has learned to nap while we're riding, and then her body lies relaxed against mine. I haven't decided yet if I enjoy it more when she's awake and talking to me, or dozing, and I can sneak in a kiss on top of her scarf-covered head.

NEHOR: Ahab and I wade through the mountain pass from Sharon into Nod. We pick our way through the rocks along the bank at the edge of the normally rushing river. Between the heat and lack of rain, the river is running unnaturally low, and so are my spirits.

The last time I crossed here I was with Mesael and Nabal on the mountain pass high above, full of high hopes. Now all I want is a change of clothes, an army, and revenge.

EGYPTUS: "So this is Shulon. It's so pretty."

"Yes," Ham agrees, "I wish I could take you south to the beach. I love it. Zaira grew up on the coast. There's always a sea breeze there, and whales, dolphins, and turtles. You could find shells to make into a necklace."

"Maybe someday we could go. A breeze sounds particularly nice right now."

It's hot, of course. We're riding through gently rolling land. Fields scattered with cows alternate with tidy, irrigated vineyards. Tall shade trees dot the landscape. It still hasn't rained, and a dusty haze hangs over everything.

Ham says, "My third father Enos lived here. He was Seth's son, who was Adam's son. Then he moved from here to the Cainan valley to live closer to sacred Mount Simeon. That's where the prophets have always gone to talk to God. He named the Cainan valley after his son Cainan."

"Will I get to see the sacred mountain?"

"Sure. The Ark is built near it, where the City of Zion was. We're just cutting across a corner of Shulon. We should be able to go over the mountain pass into Cainan in three days."

Chapter Twenty-five

NEHOR: "Gentlemen," I call out, addressing the torch-lit army before me, "this day we will right a wrong. We will retrieve a beloved daughter who has been stolen from me."

The army lets out a cheer.

"We will return Thor to Vanir the giant King."

Another cheer.

"And while we're at it, we will take possession of the most fertile of all lands -- the land of Cainan."

Big cheer.

"You know your orders. Slay the people who oppose us, enslave those who don't, and set that big ugly Ark on fire!"

Loud cheers.

"Death to Noah! "

I turn and climb on Wasp, my huge brown steed. Ahab is too tired for this foray.

My army, ten thousand strong, will surge over the mountain pass by dawn, be down the other side into Cainan by afternoon, and across the valley by evening. Noah will be dead and the Ark will provide us with a huge bonfire by tonight.

I feel the wind picking up as I lift my sword and lead the way up to the pass.

"Death to Noah!"

Ham: The wind begins as I boost Egypt onto Thor. The rabbits are safely on my back. We take nothing else but my sword and lute, the bag of gold around my neck, and the urn lid and Mehujael's stone in Egypt' pocket. All we need to do is cross over the pass of Enos from Shulon into Cainan, and ride over to the Ark. Simple. We'll be there by tonight.

I hop on Thor and reach around Egypt, who hands me the reins. While I'm at it I steal a kiss from her neck. She giggles. "Hey! We're not to the Ark yet."

"Well, we will be tonight. I wonder if Father performs evening weddings?" I can feel Egypt blush all over. She looks cute in her boy clothes, and in girl clothes. I'm still contemplating her cuteness as we head up the mountain.

We've pushed hard through Shulon, doing in two days what I was sure would take three. I think the Ark is calling Thor. He seems driven to go and go quickly, this morning especially. He's scrambling up the mountain.

We climb and climb. The wind is getting stronger the higher we go. Dawn should be breaking by now, but the sky is overcast. No sun and heat today. I'm getting more worried. Is this the day Father has been prophesying? Have we run out of time?

I groan as I see huge, black clouds rolling in from the west. Lightning is breaking in them. We are climbing higher, very close to the pass. "Go Thor!"

Whipping wind seems determined to push us off the mountain. It smells like volcano dust from Eden. It must have erupted again, more massively this time. Indeed, it would have taken a huge explosion for the dust to reach here, we're so far away now.

We're finally over the pass and darting down the descent. I continue praying, 'Oh God, we're getting there, please help us!'

NEHOR: We've crossed the mountain crevice from Nod into Cainan, and the majority of my army is on the way down, despite the fierce wind.

Massive black clouds are rolling over our heads. I've never seen darker, more menacing clouds. They suit my mood. Lightning bolts hit the ground to the west, shaking the earth and setting the drought-dry grass on fire. The troops are confused, but I charge down the mountain, leading the way, and they follow.

Now the full storm is upon us. It should be raining, but it's not. Instead, fierce lightning strikes again and again all around and among us. The earth is shaking nonstop. Boulders and landslides are rolling down the mountain, crushing soldiers and horses. Fire erupts everywhere. Chaos. The troops are scattering.

Wasp rears up and I cling to him. He bolts and we leave the mountain behind. I try to direct him to the Ark. It's way across the valley, but at this speed...Death to Noah!

EGYPTUS: I have my eyes closed. The smoke from the fires is choking me, burning my eyes if I open them.

The ground is shaking. Thor is dashing down the incline and I am praying at full speed. Ham is holding all four of us on the horse.

"We're at the bottom of the mountain!" Ham calls. I squint my eyes open. Black, burning hell. Thor seems to know where he's headed: straight into it.

I feel the rain start, only it's not rain, it's giant balls of hail stinging as they land on me. It's going to kill everything out in the open. We're going to die.

NEHOR: Army or no army, vengeance is mine. I'm near the towering Ark, but the door is closed.

Hail is pelting me, and I draw my sword in defiance. Raising it high, I charge the ship. I hear a crash and lightning descends down my blade.

HAM: The hail has stopped and sheets of rain are now pelting us, clearing the choking smoke and volcano dust. Thor keeps tearing along. I see the Ark: large and looming, visible clearly with the bright lightning strikes.

We're getting nearer. Bless Thor, he just keeps going and going, splashing through the now-sodden ground.

The Ark is closer still, but the door is shut. God has closed up the heavy door, just as Father said he would. We're too late. So close, but too late. Thor is still racing full speed. We're closer, closer. Egypt is hanging on. I can tell she's still praying. The irony is we're going to make it to the Ark, but we won't be able to enter.

I look again. Is the drawbridge-like door cracked open? The opening is wider, wider still. Thor knows exactly where he's going. The portal hits the ground with a thud as we arrive and Thor bolts up it and in. We made it! Thor is my hero. Egypt is sobbing with relief.

The big door begins creaking closed again behind us. Six people are jumping and cheering as we're pulled off the shaking, soaking horse. Japheth is the first to hug me.

"Careful, rabbits," I say with a joyous laugh.

"Rabbits?" I hand him my pack and he gently takes it and looks inside to greet our travel-weary friends.

Smiling, he carries them away to find a nest in the Ark. Father's next with a tearful, laughing hug; then sweet Mother, who clings tightly and kisses my face; tall, handsome Shem; beautiful Roseta.

"Where's Zaira?"

Shem replies, "She took Egyptus upstairs to bathe and get a dry gown on. They'll be back. He pats Thor's side. Let's get Thor brushed down and settled, then you need to come look over here. Your horse Midnight arrived a few days ago and came aboard."

Chapter Twenty-six

EGYPTUS: I've bathed and dressed, and feel a tremor go
through the Ark as I sit on a stool bundled in a blanket. I'm
warming up at last. Zaira is combing my finally-clean, unbraided
hair. It has taken a while to wash away the journey's grime and
soot. Roseta brought us in a much-appreciated tray loaded with
hot tea and snacks, and stayed to eat with us. I gave her
Mahujael's message, which made her very happy, and she's
promised to tell me all about her tutor.

      We are up on the Ark's third level in Ham's
compartment. I would have known it was his without being told,

because the walls are covered with pegs from which hang very fine musical instruments collected from his travels. It seems that more than just animals will survive the flood.

There are no windows in this huge ship, but the inside is lit up by white, glowing rocks mounted on the walls. "Noah brought them from Mount Simeon," Zaira tells me. "He says he and God agreed it would be better than being in the dark."

Roseta is sitting cross-legged on the bed, watching Zaira's art unfold on my head. She says, "When the animals all marched up into the Ark last night and the door closed, we were afraid it was too late. We've been fasting and praying for your arrival ever since."

I reply gratefully, "We needed all your prayers. We wouldn't have made it without God's guiding hand. By the way, for a ship full of animals, it was really quiet down there."

"Yes," Roseta replies, " Noah says most of the animals will hibernate, or sleep through the trip. We couldn't bring enough food to feed them all, or have them eating each other."

Zaira's busy hands pause and she steps back. "Stand up."

Annah and the girls had faith that I was coming and had fun picking out and making lots of beautiful clothes for me, long enough for my tall body.

I stand and take off the blanket. The two girls look me up and down. My silky dress is a gentle, light mossy green with a pink flower pattern embroidered on it. There's a wide pink belt around my waist and matching green embroidered shoes, which are actually big enough for my long feet. It's a day of miracles.

Zaira has pulled my hair up and back and secured it with wire pins topped with artfully crafted pink flowers.

"You look like a beautiful queen," She says.

"You really do," agrees Rose.

"Thank you." I feel an instant friendship with charming, blond, blue-eyed Zaira and exquisite, voluptuous, dark-haired Roseta. The three of us couldn't look less alike, but they feel like sisters to me. We smile at each other.

"Wait," Zaira says and opens a small box on the little table. She holds it out to me. My mother's earrings! The green stones shine as I pick them up.

"Thank you mama," I whisper and my eyes become moist. I feel she is here with me. I fasten them on, realizing that Annah and the girls must have picked out this whole outfit to match the earrings.

"Now you look complete," Zaira says. "Let's go find Ham. Noah is anxious to officiate at your wedding. After all, we didn't build you a separate compartment."

I'm still blushing as we head down the passageway on the third level, which has the family's rooms, and enter the forward part of the ship where all are waiting. Noah has changed into his spectacular blue and gold preaching clothes, but I only have eyes for Ham.

He's wearing shiny new brown boots with leggings to match. His embroidered tunic is dark green with a brown leather belt. Bathed and shaved, with his hair combed back, his handsome blue eyes are full of love for me. He looks truly, completely happy.

He reaches both hands out for mine and I step forward and take them.

"Kneel, my children," Noah invites. We do, continuing to hold hands, facing each other. Ham's hands are so warm. He gives my trembling ones a little squeeze.

As we tenderly look into each others' beloved eyes, Noah says, "On this night when the world outside is dying, we celebrate hope for future life on this earth, and the knowledge that God's love and goodness can be carried in our hearts and actions."

He then begins our marriage ceremony, and the sacred words penetrate into my heart. Ham's voice is certain when he says, "I will," as he gives himself to me as husband. Mine is shaking with happy tears but I manage a sincere, "I will," and I am his wife.

Ham leans forward to kiss me. As his lips cover mine, his kiss is as delicious and precious as I've been remembering during the weeks since we left Eden. Ham lifts his head and suddenly the ship moves again. We tilt one way, then another. I cling to my new spouse.

Noah straightens himself and announces, "I think we might have a rough bit for a while as the ship is lifted up by the rising flood. We'd probably all be safer in our beds."

Ham gives me a wry smile. "Oh, I think we can manage that."

I nod and reply with a straight face, "Yes, I think we can."

The End

Questions for Reflection:

1. Egyptus is aware of her father's faults but loves him anyway. How have your parents' faults affected your feelings for them?

2. Egyptus and Ham know that they love each other and share values and goals. What do they do to strengthen their bond?

3. The people either ignore or reject Noah's message, even when they see the animals heading to the Ark. Why do they do this when it turns out to be so important?

4. Though they live and interact in a sinful society, Noah and the believers behave differently because of their values. How have your values affected the way you live?

5. Egyptus would like to bring her sister Zillah to the Ark. Whom would you bring?

6. When Egyptus meets Roseta and Zaira, they are instantly friends. Have you ever felt like that when you've met a friend?

About the Author:

M.M. Robison graduated from Brigham Young University with a Bachelor's degree in English. She now plans to continue writing and thinks of life as an adventure, because you never really know what's going to happen next. Visit her at: MMRobison.com

About the Illustrator:

Encouraged as a child to be creative, Melanie A. Murphy always enjoyed sewing and crafts, but didn't begin painting until she was really grown up. She believes true art in any form comes from the soul and that training in technique lets the artist more fully express herself or himself. View more of her art at: MMRobison.com

Patrick A. Murphy, a talented professor and photographer, did the art photography. He and Kim Murphy, a gifted web design teacher, did the cover layout.

Sincere thanks go to Bethanie for technical support. Many thanks also go to Don and Carolyn for every other kind of support, and to all of the manuscript readers.